Roses are Red, Violets are Stealing Loose Change from my Pockets While I Sleep

By David S. Atkinson

Literary Wanderlust, Denver, Colorado

Dedication

For Biggles, and all his adventures in time.

There's a rabbit living under my kitchen sink...

There's a rabbit that lives under my sink in the kitchen. He built a nest out of quarks and gravitons down there at the back behind my tools, cleaning products, and grocery bags. He has shag fur and diesel fuel for blood.

To the casual observer, he would look more like a penguin. They'd think: *Hey, that's a penguin with shag for fur and diesel fuel for blood living in that quark and graviton nest under that guy's sink.* However, I know it's really a rabbit.

The rabbit knows a secret passage under the sink that leads into my walls. During the day he reads a copy of *Bridget Jones's Diary* he has in his nest, but at night he slides on his belly into the secret passage and slithers around. I can hear it. I can hear him chewing on celery that the government sends him. He slides into the space in the wall behind my bed and whispers to me while I sleep. He whispers secrets from books about the old gods and the time before the universe was born. Books written by blind, mad monks who saw too much. Books revealing things man was never meant to know. He whispers secrets about the time before time to drive me mad.

I don't know how the rabbit knows that stuff. All he reads is that damn *Bridget Jones's Diary*. At least he's not whispering things from that at night. Then I really would go mad.

The rabbit doesn't like it when I talk to the bum down the street, the one that lives under parked cars and eats discarded mint dental floss. He asks me if I have spare change when I see him. That's to let me know that he knows I know about the symbols hidden on improperly stamped souvenir Alcatraz coins. He knows I walk toward the west on alternate Sundays in Tucson.

He told me about his brother's goldmine, a way to extract it from sagebrush out in Colorado. He discovered the secret by listening to vibrations from his fillings. That's why he insisted on the silver amalgam. The polymer invisible ones don't vibrate right.

The CIA took the mine away, though. His brother had filed his claim and everything, filed it in a dentist's office instead of the land survey to throw them off, but they found out anyway. They redrew the maps with crayon so it was in Wyoming instead of Utah. Then he couldn't find it.

The bum knows I can help. I know about longitudes and latitudes.

The rabbit doesn't like it when I talk to the bum. He knows the bum would share the gold with me if I helped get the mine back. Then I could line my walls and not hear the rabbit whisper secrets at night. Then I'd be free from him.

I'm not worried, though. Even if I don't get the goldmine back, I can always pretend to be a cola. Everyone knows that cola is a rabbit's greatest fear. Have you ever seen a rabbit drink a cola? You haven't because rabbits fear cola more than anything else.

Even more than plastic wrap.

I've got that rabbit under control. I'll let him whisper some…just to learn a few things. If I get tired of it or need to sleep, I'll just pretend to be a cola. That'd show him. That'd show any rabbit.

Easily Train at Home to Sell No Money Down Real Estate Related to Your Own Home Relative Trepanning Operation, But Keep in Mind That Billy Mays Overdosed on OxiClean When Someone Slipped Him Purer Stuff Than Usual

My parents were only making noise when they talked rather than saying words again, so they must have once more been reconsidering selling my limbs to the gypsies. They've weighed the pros and cons so often, me listening in each time whether I wanted to or not, that they tore right through the sound membrane of that particular conversation and ruined any acoustical sense that once was there. Like all adults in a Charlie Brown special really, but most particularly like Adlai Stevenson's address at the United Nations about engendered British Truffle Waffles during the Congolese convenience store wars of 1976.

No matter, we'd heard it all before. Always.

I mean, I could probably have repeated the whole conversation verbatim if I hadn't pulled my brain out as a single long strand through my nose with that electric spaghetti fork. Even still, I was sure I had the gist. Dad was in favor of the sale, citing my lack of skills with a baseball, but mom thought having no limbs would make me a lot of trouble.

Dad said let me keep one or two then, preferably ones that wouldn't let me follow him around and bother him, but mom said then we wouldn't get the package premium and/or the free Panasonic microwave.

I think mom was holding out for a selection sale that included the microwave, rate be damned, but I could have been wrong.

Every time the subject came up, when the words became shrieks and scratches and clicks and bells and tones, I got out of the house for a while, made myself scarce. I volunteered for one-man square-dancing recycling missions to the other side of Planet Hollywood's spare moon. I joined up with the French Foreign Legion and asked them to post me at KISS concerts on the Eastern seaboard. I studied hard and got into a good school and became an ears/nose/throat doctor with a thriving practice in Baltimore and a wonderful wife who gave birth to two lovely children all before I ditched them for a low-effort life drinking cheap pilsner beer with a guy named Morty by telling my family and co-workers that I'm really a Freon delivery man named Earl who came to read the toothpaste meter. You know, whatever to kill some time until the danger to my limbs had passed.

I planned on keeping those if I could.

It always blew over sooner or later. I'd come back and the words would be flowing again. It had to, the gypsies confided to me over Kraft macaroni & cheese that the whole limb purchase offer was a practical joke and they hadn't had the heart to come clean once my parent got so excited.

Still, I would have rested easier if they hadn't discussed it so often.

If the Judge Doesn't Specifically Discuss Passing Go or Collecting $200 as Part of Reading my Sentence Then That Backhoe Hole I Dug Will Have Been Totally Worth it

Escape tunnels seemed like a smart idea when I got started, but I began to reconsider after a while. Having to get tags and insurance for each got expensive, and Cormac McCarthy was always trying to borrow one or more. Perhaps I should have just gotten ninja smoke bombs from the back of that magazine at the mall and learned to disappear instead. You know, like Don Herbert.

After all, who knew where all you'd want to escape to? Or, for that matter, from? One from my office to home was nice, but then I had to consider the times when I wanted to stop by Vic's Corn Popper on the way. That happened often enough, so I needed one from the office to there…and then from there to home to avoid having to backtrack.

We won't even talk about the days I wanted to take the scenic route, or grab coffee.

Soon, those escape tunnels were everywhere. Subsidence was an issue. Shell tried drilling for oil in one, and Leonard Peltier took up residence in a few others. Putting Leonard up for a bit was the least I could do for him, but screw Shell and their refusal to let me run naked through their car wash. Regardless, both made using my escape tunnels more problematic. I mean, how could I just zip through without stopping to treat Leonard to juice and cake?

As if.

I got Ross Perot to build the things for me, but even that had its issues. For one thing, did you know he's not dead yet? I sure didn't, had to check. You wouldn't believe how that held up finalization of the contract. Only about half as long as the fact he turned out to never have gotten elected president of the *Army of Darkness* film appreciation and doughnut cooking society, but still.

Still ended up with tunnels running all over the place, constant construction.

Eventually, I ended up licensing it all to Elon Musk and went back to using normal roads. Between Mole Man, the Moloids, and the rest of the daily commuters, it was simply too crowded and an ordinary sedan was just faster. Turned out, most people could dig and found the tunnels anyway, loving shortcuts as much as they did. Totally wasted my time, and all my Jell-O, with the whole endeavor.

So not worth it.

Just Talk Louder Then Kick Them in the Balls

I was freaked out and all visiting the Catacombs in Paris, wandering through the dark limestone tunnels of piled up bones until I accidentally walked through a metal door and found the staff faking skulls out of sugar and recycled Mighty Dog tins. They admitted when sufficiently pressed that it'd been a sham from the start. It was all a rumor originated by Hemingway and Stein to make Paris seem cooler and the citizens decided to roll with it instead of opening a new Six Flags.

No one had ever caught on, they said.

Worse, I realized they were all talking in South Jersey accents as they went on. Turned out, the whole country was a fake now, a theme park run by out of work American carneys and hard luck door-to-door kitchenware salesmen. There hadn't been any actual French since the last war. Not that they'd died or anything — they simply lost interest in being French and went back to school to learn VCR repair.

Specialized in Betamax, apparently, so things hadn't gone real well. Still, actors had taken over to keep up appearances and everyone lost track of where the real French had gone.

Des Moines maybe.

I thought for sure they'd kill me to protect their secret, guard the hell of a cash cow they had going there. But they said they weren't worried. With all the money they made licensing baguette and beret rights around the world, there was no actual need to keep the park up anymore. If it all came out they'd finally get a weekend off, though they still kept at it to not disappoint all the high school Francophile girls around the world. I could tell if I wanted or not, but that was up to me.

Of course, they did break my ribs smacking me around with day-old croissants and paperback copies of *Les Misérables*. That was simply for fun though, something to do until their next shift standing around on a street corner looking surly and smoking tiny cigarettes.

I kept my mouth shut either way. That villa I bought in Provence wouldn't be worth squat if I blabbed, and I'd never get enough money to compete in the International Bubble Gum Chewing and Cross Stitch Championships if that investment fell flat. Whistle blowing wouldn't have done anyone any good.

I did cut my trip short though. Why pay to see people pretend to be French? I can check out that sort of thing any time for free in the Whole Foods wine section at home, or Costco by the toilet paper.

I mean, as if.

Communist Agents in the Government Regularly Swap Labor and Memorial Days to See if Anyone is Paying Attention

Long weekends always screw me up at work. For example, after getting last Monday and Tuesday off for the Turgor Pressure Awareness holiday, I forgot where I was employed. Seriously, I got up and stole a 73 Honda hatchback to drive downtown like normal, but I had no idea where to go once I got there.

Was I a toaster refurbisher? Did I clean used Cap'n Crunch decoder rings for the Chinese? Perhaps I was a nuclear research assistant and grant application procrastinator at the new Huffy mountain bike positron collider in the California Street light rail station. Nothing was ringing a bell…was I a bell ringer?

I remembered where I usually dumped the cars in the alley behind the 7–Eleven and bikini wax studio, but nothing after that. All the office buildings seemed foreign, like when Andy Dick faked his death to start a simpler life as a ballpark hotdog vendor at a Mafia cart in the Amana Colonies. Taking a page from old Andy's playbook though, I simply picked one at random.

Didn't he say 90% of success was showing up? It was either him or Lamont Cranston.

I did get a few funny looks when I wandered into an empty office and sat down. Must have been the wrong building, but who were those people to judge? They didn't know me. At least, I think they didn't. I have to admit, the "no water cooler sponge bath" rule at wherever I did work had made me a bit antisocial most of the time. Perhaps I wouldn't have recognized my co-workers even if I guessed right, which it was still possible I had.

A woman named Linda stormed in demanding to know if I'd completed the Blain opinion. That sounded like bullshit, so I pressed my luck. I said she was crazy, that I was her boss and was waiting for her to get it done. She replied she was pretty sure it was the other way around, but wanted to be sensitive to my point of view.

Turns out, she'd forgotten where she worked and wandered in randomly too. We ended up shooting the breeze for a while and refinished the office furniture using a discarded emery board and a pastrami sandwich. No one seemed to care, so it was even harder to speculate what kind of business was normally done there. Our bet was on oil and gas leasing, but then it was five and time to go home.

Honestly, nice as an extra day or two off is, it simply ruins my productivity until I'm back for a couple days. I'm getting good results on the credenza with the muenster on the sandwich, but National Groin Band-Aid Shaving Preparation Day of Remembrance is right around the corner. That'll just throw me off all over again.

Even Chuck Norris Fears the Wrath of 13-Word and His Band of Misshapen Ferrets

My daughter asked me to tell her a 13-Word story the other day. Normally I would have just told her to get back to work sewing those War of 1812 leather key chains with the discovery of intermittent windshield wiper snow globes attached that I sell at the rest stop outside Phoenix, but this was 13-Word we were talking about. 13-Word is a bad motherfucker, and he's been known to mess up dudes who don't show the proper respect when telling their daughter stories.

How do you think people found out about the break-in at the Watergate Hotel? Sure, the official story has something to do with a security guard noticing some taped doors, a big press investigation by *Boy's Life*, but that all led back to 13-Word. Nixon really should have known better than to finish the last of 13-Word's milk without buying a new carton. Library fine jail cellmates just don't do that.

Men on the inside have been killed for less.

Who do you think put FDR into that cybernetic Twizzlers exoskeleton? Who do you think replaced the bricks of the pyramids with high-impact thermal rubber Monte Cristo sandwiches? Who do you think took the U.S. off the gold standard so he could impress Helen of Troy with all those ingots?

It sure wasn't 13-Word's little brother Terrence, no matter what the KGB frame-up transcripts say. We *all* know better.

Heck, even the origins of 13-Word are shrouded in deepest cellophane mystery. Some say he was on a routine Ford Expedition when he met the greatest earthquake ever known, which was high on freebasing Desenex at the time, and the Colorado Rapids struck his tiny raft, plunging him a thousand cubic feet below where he was granted the powers of four out of five dentists. Personally, I don't believe that. It sounds too much like a cheap TV show theme song, and haters just hating.

After all, would 13-Word have knocked out the 1916 polio epidemic with one punch if it were true? Even if it did scuff his flip-flops? No, clearly, he must have obtained mutant abilities by going over the bar on that cursed swing set at the Camp David parade grounds and traveled back in time to the medieval village of Hamburg at the precise moment necessary to prevent the invention of nylon bedazzled hip waders.

That's the only explanation that makes sense.

Don't tell that to my daughter though. She won't buy it. Maybe I shouldn't have fed her all those leftover key chains over the years after they'd expired so I couldn't sell them anymore.

I think that's what killed her ability to believe. Also, probably her liver.

Less Than a Hundred Words that Left Your Wavy Lover

In less than 100 words, she told me we couldn't be together, words including "sprocket" and "moist" and "Wankel rotary engine."

She said the A-Team was curing ice cream headache in Uganda by time traveling to prevent its birth, that Blue Bonnet hired the IRA to stop them. She said eating printed circuit boards caused incurable shoe cancer, that Henry and Jane Fonda were anti-matter versions of each other, that we'll all die in a freak zeppelin/watermelon suspender accident.

In less than 100 words, she told me she was a broken AM radio that I'd mistaken for my girlfriend yet again.

The Revolutionaries Denounced Anyone with more than 20,000 Frequent Flyer Miles Because Upgrades are the Complimentary Beverages of the Flying Public

I found out I was royalty on a recent connecting flight from Burbank to Albuquerque. It isn't the sort of thing one normally expects from air travel, but they've added so many optional frills these days. I suppose I shouldn't have been surprised; forget to uncheck one opt-out five-dollar upcharge and you're of noble blood.

Typical.

The truth came out during takeoff. I just needed to recline my chair for a second so I could finish my hydrazine/Mountain Dew sponge bath. I was going to put it right back, I swear. All of a sudden, the whole plane was in an uproar.

Apparently, it isn't that you aren't supposed to put tray tables down or recline seats during takeoff and landing…it's that no one *can*. Some kind of mystical force is involved, like mitosis. The fact I did it meant that I was the promised one, foretold in legends found at the back of the safety card inside the provided seat pocket.

Who knew?

The discovery was pretty sweet. I got immediately bumped up to first class and even got a free adult beverage out of the deal. I still had to pay for my snack pack, but Christian Slater showed up using the Shroud of Turin as a toga to unwrap everything and feed it to me by hand. That's usually extra.

I worried a bit about what I'd been prophesied to do,

but apparently, it only involved opening the exit doors in the event of a water landing. Given the droughts in California recently, I didn't think there was much chance it would ever come up. Even if it did, I still wasn't worried. I could always just abdicate like Katharine Hepburn.

I mean, there are established procedures for those sorts of things and that's exactly why.

Buying All the Junk in the Back of *Boys' Life* at Once Would Yield the Weirdest Post-Apocalyptic Society Saturday Morning Cartoon Show Ever

Answering ads from comic books to make extra money is a hit or miss proposition. Some kids end up hawking junk for the Olympic Sales Club, but others like me and Colin Powell end up Nepalese crime lords named Twenty-One (something about either body counts, genital size, and/or the number of seconds into a conversation we could go without making a reference to Pee-wee Herman). You'd think there's no way it could happen the same way to both of us, but comic book ads are never what they appear to be.

And you never listen to the way your parents try to warn you.

Sure, it starts simple enough. All you have to do is send twenty-five cents through the mail to get plans for a fuel-free potato gun. Then you're knocking over a post office though with Jennifer Grey because you *can't* send change through the United States mail. Then, when you find out the quarter was just for the informational pamphlet on buying the actual plans and the crew from the original *Ghostbusters* movie along with the two or three from the new one who were willing to stoop to the job start coming around to slash your bike tires and let you know a little more is going to be required from you, that's when you get to taking out banks real heavy.

All to get your potato gun, which turns out to be disappointing enough on its own even before you find out that this finally-granted favor means that there will be other, even less savory duties for you.

Helpful tip: Wells Fargo doesn't actually have any real money inside the bank. All the hardcore bank robbers know this and you'll look like a total fool if you go in expecting to find any. Some genius hybrid Welshman came up with a fee structure for them guaranteeing they'd never have to pay any deposited money back, something about amortized mortgage futures of a dairy cow named Albert, so they just go ahead and immediately spend any dollars they get. Bankers actually run out in the middle of a transaction to buy Nilla Wafers and bottles of MD 20/20. It's true.

Bottom line, pick another financial institution.

Anyway, then there was a whole bunch of stuff about taking on the Liechtenstein bicycle mafia, running X-ray specs with Jerry Maguire out of Belize, assassinating a bunch of deceased celebrities using calls to the Psychic Friends Network, and so on. That was all pretty boring, so I'll spare you the details.

Suffice it to say, you might want to give that comic ad a pass…or stick to the one for the Olympic Sales Club.

This Song is Just As Annoying as it Ever Was, But Now I Screwed up the Rhythm and Sold the Rights to Pakistan

A hundred bottles of beer on the wall, a hundred bottles of beer! Well, BuzzFeed reported there were a hundred. Clarence Thomas urged people not to rely on the exact number without a scientific inquiry and nineteen months of independent peer-reviewed dairy snacks, but no one listened. The other news outlets merely stated that BuzzFeed reported a number, which might or might not have been one hundred. Take one down and pass it around and Eugene O'Neill would remind you that you have a purported ninety-nine bottles of beer on the wall but still can't be sure due to the original uncertainty.

Ninety-nine bottles of beer on the wall, ninety-nine bottles of beer! Fine, the 1986 Olympic committee asked, just for the sake of argument and old socks, that we assume there were originally a hundred bottles of beer on the wall. Reports had surfaced that the hundredth bottle, described in the paragraph above as taken down and passed around, was broken by Bonnie Franklin obtaining glass shards to be used to castrate Ron Jeremy. However, that turned out to only be old *Mister Ed* fan fiction put out on 4chan. As such, Muammar Gaddafi himself took a bottle down and passed it around. Ninety-eight bottles of beer on the wall!

Ninety-eight bottles of beer on the wall, ninety-eight bottles of beer! Take one down, pass it around, black out and forget how many beers precisely had been drunk, wake up in Reno covered in stale elf blood with Steve Carell and the original motorcycle used by Peter Fonda as part of that dominatrix scene in *Pee-wee's Big Adventure,* try to rub off that risqué tattoo of Ed Meese in a denim jacket, and try to count the remaining beer to see how much remains. Twelve bottles of beer on the wall!

Twelve bottles of beer on the wall, twelve bottles of beer! Try to take one down and pass it around only to get told by Ed Hardy that they're all being aged as "private reserve." Seriously, does everything have to be done *craft* anymore? Can't people just have basic stuff and enjoy that without getting the ATF involved in every American Legion Post #235 bikini swimsuit lookalike calendar raffle contest? Apparently not, still twelve bottles of beer on the wall!

Eternal Insult Comics and Postal Forwarding Claim Forms

Some thought it would come from the Bible, others through a plague. Pretty much everyone was caught off guard though when the Apocalypse came in the mail. But there it was, all wrapped up in partially used bubble wrap and covered in brown paper so as to be discreet.

The end of the world.

To be honest, most weren't aware that there even was mail anymore. Those boxes on the front of their houses only spawned advertising circulars for neighborhood motorcycle swap meets and samples of biodegradable honey baked ham, so they thought it was some kind of physical conduit connected to their cable television services. The idea that it was somehow related to governmental shipment of packages and other messages was a real revelation…just like Revelations.

But the Armageddon had arrived that way regardless.

A few thought about sending it back, marking the addressee deceased and leaving it on their porches again, but there were no longer any postal carriers to claim it. The world had ended, returns no longer possible. Worse, the end had come postage due…though the lack of consequences that could be inflicted made it wildly unlikely that anyone had paid, other than perhaps Perry Mason due to his inflexible sense of fair play. Who else would feel like paying without possible penalties? And with what would they pay?

The afterlife is not subject to garnishment, or delivery of process for lawsuit.

A few officials, such as Ari Fleischer and Phyllis Schlafly, might have objected to the whole setup. After all, it was a violation of postal regulations to send harmful materials through the mail…and what could be more harmful than the Apocalypse? However, since civil authority ended with the world, much like the hierarchy of Vatican milk labeling standards, the malefactors went unpunished.

By secular hands, at least.

I tell you, it's a good thing I don't check my mail. Me and Don Rickles, along with his pet fish Fluffy, are the only ones left. We're just kind of floating in nothing here, kept company by twenty crates of industrial spray cheese. Of course, I might resort to checking my mail too, ending it all, if Don doesn't shut up pretty soon here. He just won't seem to give it a rest, no matter how much I beg.

It's enough to drive a man over the edge.

Doctor Octal Goes to Washington to Reclaim the Aleutian Islands

I was watching one of those nightmare sweet sixteen shows the other day. The girl involved burned down a Starbucks and a 7–Eleven because her parents brought peace to Yemen instead of the Ukraine like she'd wanted. No status in Yemen I guess, but she flipped her lid regardless. Ended up sentenced to twenty years in cracker jail (where the worst of the Triscuits are incarcerated), but it got me thinking. I figured I should have my own sweet sixteen party.

After all, I'd never had one. That probably related to me being a forty-year-old balding man in Saint Louis who was dropped off by his parents one day at Space Camp and never reclaimed because I'd never pick up my room, my parents eschewing all forms of confrontation, but still. I wanted one. All the guys at the office had one recently.

So, I threw one myself. Got a white dress, though it looked a bit more like a ratty powder blue Nike track suit with burn holes in the armpits. Also ordered a cake, though that more closely resembled a half-drunk plastic gallon of Black Velvet. Working on a budget sucks.

I'm only so good at throwing parties.

It went well, however. I invited all my friends. Mr. Roper, JJ Walker, Gilligan (though I gave the Skipper a miss), Michael Knight, David Banner, the waitresses from *Cheers*, everybody came. Or, at least that's who they said they were. They looked a lot like the 1985 Packers offensive line, but many years have passed since then. It's kind of hard to recognize people these days.

Still, we marked my coming of age as a young adult woman all right. My guests all did my hair and makeup and tattooed my back with a precise scale model of the ceiling of the Sistine Chapel, or at least how it would look rendered on an Atari 2600 by Max Headroom. Good times, good times.

Of course, Gloria Steinem and Phyllis Schlafly did beat

the living crap out of me with a motorcycle chain and a broken Chivas Regal bottle. I had to expect that, so I wasn't too upset. Didn't let it spoil my big day.

It's simply the mark of a good sweet sixteen party so I was glad it happened at mine.

"X" Marks the Spot Unless You Use a Little Club Soda

Dear "Editor": I must object, in the strongest terms possible, to the repeated and unconscionable use of the letter "X" in many articles of the September twenty-seventh issue of your newspaper. Such an action is frighteningly irresponsible, particularly for a publication as highly respected as the *North Lansing Sanitary Improvement District Eight News* and Classified Bowling Advertisements, and I can only imagine that you are not reviewing your newspaper in any fashion before it goes to print.

In case the situation has in fact escaped your supervisory notice, "X" represents an unknown. This convention is followed throughout many branches of mathematics, sciences, and even social sciences, which are much like the other sciences but with substantially more parties.

Do you simply not care what "X" may represent? Have you even considered the danger? "X" could represent anything!

What if "X" turned out to stand for a terrorist? Do you really think it appropriate to have terrorists infiltrating your article about the president meeting with Gilligan and the Skipper at the White House Rose Garden to discus coconut exchange agreements with T.J. Maxx franchises in the Northern Yukon Territories? You may have inadvertently put terrorists in the White House! Did you bother to check? Are you at all concerned?

Such lax oversight hardly speaks well of your commitment to running a reliable news source.

Even if you wish to remain so cavalier about use of "X," why not take the precaution of defining it? Would that take so much time away from your cruising the Mall of America for underage Doberman traders? It seems that this would be the least you could do.

For example, within the context of this letter, let it be known that "X" is defined as Charles Lindbergh as the gross national product of the Denver Mattress Company approaches morbid obesity from silicon glass jars of organic lime-flavored parboiled pig knuckles. See how easy that was? One sentence and we are fully apprised of any potential threats, the situation completely controlled.

However you decide best to handle this matter in future, I must demand you address it in some way. We cannot allow communists into our wedding announcements or sheep philanderers in our supermarket coupon inserts. Please, consider renewing your vows to responsible journalism or I will be forced to cancel my free and unrequested subscription in the interests of public safety.

Sincerely,

Xander Xybold Xmith, xylophone enthusiast emeritus

Vidal Sassoon Once Cut Bob Ross During a Street Fight in Rio Over a Pair of Decorative Ball-Peen Tack Hammers

I grew hair on the walls of my living room. What else could I do? After Donald Knuth hosted that special edition of *MTV Cribs*, simply painting and wallpapering didn't cut it anymore. Wall hangings weren't even to be talked about. It seemed every jerk on Walnut Street had a Van Gogh now that those Nigerian princes finally started paying out.

Getting it started wasn't too hard. I simply rubbed the drywall with that Rogaine shampoo once a week and things started sprouting. Of course, it only worked after I'd held it in my mouth long enough to leach out all the sodium laureth sulfate. I may have ruined at least three of my kidneys that way, but my walls look great.

All the door-to-door RV tire salesmen say so.

Sure, I've got to shampoo and condition my living room twice a week, but that's not too much trouble. The brushing and braiding is actually kind of soothing. Barrettes make for a neat look, and I use the one with the glass clackers when company is coming, open up the windows so the wind gets a whole concert going.

It's a heck of a show, though I am considering having it all permed.

My biggest problem is actually Tom Selleck. He keeps sneaking into the house and making off with large swaths of the walls to pass off as his own body hair. Few would believe it, but he's cue bald from the neck down ever since him and John Hillerman got into that tweezers fight on the set years ago after they huffed an entire can of Aqua Net. He's pretty embarrassed about it, which I guess I would be too.

Higgins got away without a scratch.

Still, I wish he'd leave my walls alone. I've already got a circus crew coming next week to look at my den. There are simply other rooms in my house for me to get to and I need the living room to stay done.

Professional Wrestling is a Lie Jimmy Carter Told Us About the Second Gunman to Cover for the Vacation the Trilateral Commission Took to Teletubby Island Last Fall

The snow was all around me, but it was actually a pretty warm day. Upper eighties, I think. The swirling flakes were all plastic, so it's not as if it needed to be cold or anything. It was all part of a normal day since President for Life Hulk Hogan sealed Washington D.C. in a giant bubble and filled it with shredded white grocery bags. Shook it once in a while, usually at least daily.

The Hulkster liked a snow globe.

The current situation stemmed from that "sex" tape that "news" site released of him. Groper or Grouper or The Pink Floyd Wall Street Journal, something like that. He got a pretty big judgment against them, though I don't remember the precise cause of action. Maybe invasion of privacy, or lewd acts with a duck of the underage opposite sex after seven p.m. on the East Coast. All I knew is he got a lot: all their money, the continental United States, the solid state of matter, a plastic chess set, and even eight different types of theoretical atomic particles.

Hell of a lawyer the Hulk had there.

So, he declared himself President for Life and started working on a few changes. Even he didn't know how a court could award him things the defendant didn't own, but he went with it and didn't ask questions…much like when Bobby the Brain Heenan slipped on the Whole Foods produce section outside Philly in the middle of that '83 steel cage match and knocked himself unconscious.

Total rookie move. I mean, that was the *first* thing you train to handle.

But anyway, cage, court, "sex tape," snow globe. It all lined up and that was why I had to clear my front walk with a combination riding vacuum cleaner/industrial grade Easy-Bake Oven. After all, it's not as if that crap is going to melt.

Trust me, it never does.

Extreme Couponing Can Yield a Month's Worth of Existential Dread for Less Than Three Dollars Canadian

I went to the store the other day because my city needed a new mayor. The old one was getting somewhat worn out and would start chirping every eight hours, no matter how often we replaced the nine-volt battery or pressed reset. Besides, King Soopers was running a sale on political figures, and it was double coupon day…though only if you had their "Rule, Britannia!" themed saver's card.

Mind you, even with the sale I still wanted to do a little price comparison. Not all mayors are created equal, and what at first seems to be the best deal might not actually be the greatest value.

I mean, you can't just assume the high-class brand mayors in their fancy little political end cap displays are better just because of their flashy packaging and known brand reputation. Sometimes they are more reliable than the generic mayoral equivalent, but not always. It may even be the case that generic mayors are only the high-class ones repackaged in more casual clothes…at half the cost.

You have to check. Why pay extra only for a mayor's name?

Also, the budget line off over on the beaten-up, half-empty shelves with most of their paint worn away may seem shoddy, but there are surprises there too. Verify the mayor cost per unit there. It's a frequent practice to dilute budget mayors, sometimes with as much as seventy-percent state senator, to the point that you actually end up paying more for the same amount of mayor. They sometimes gamble on you thinking you'll save because they shove them into cheap bags rather than even using any cardboard boxes.

We won't even talk about performance there. Just remember to look at the Amazon reviews first.

Though, all that careful shopping ended up being for naught anyway. I stuck my mayor in that rack under the cart and didn't notice the clerk missed scanning it when I went through, making my mayor a hundred percent free anyway. I'd have gone for a more full-featured mayor if I'd known, but who could have seen that coming...or the subsequent marmoset flood?

I'll just keep that in mind when I go to the video store to select a new community college board next week. We may have a bigger budget for that due to the artificial typewriter industry payola kickbacks, but no budget is infinite.

Kleinfeld's Krampus Was Not as Big a Draw as Their Easter Bunny Even Though They Offered a Free Veil With Dress Purchase if he Kidnapped Your Children in a Sack

There was a hole in the woodwork around the window seat of my bed and breakfast room in Glenwood Springs, Colorado, so I started squirting toothpaste in there. I guess it just felt like a natural thing to do after binge-watching the seventeenth annual electric hopscotch championships for hemorrhoid sufferers, but regardless it's what I did. The hole looked like it led into somewhere deep below, somewhere that went down quite a ways, and I had the toothpaste in my hand already. What else was I supposed to use to investigate?

Maybe I should have just shone the flashlight on my phone in there instead.

The first tube went in with no problem. Didn't even need time to drip down. The next one hundred and forty-three were pretty much the same; I always traveled with a gross. Beyond that, I had to start asking room service for additional tubes. Luckily, most places give out toothpaste as a complimentary item, just in case people forget. I'd have gone broke faster than I did if there had been any kind of charge. The paste went through the hole so quick that I had to stay on the line continuously to beg for more, one hand squeezing the current tube while the other held the phone I used to ask for the next. It was monotonous but made me glad I hadn't let Paul Hogan eat one of my arms after all when we were in that E. coli burger return line at Jack in the Box. Turned out I really needed both for the toothpaste thing, and Paul wasn't really hypoglycemic after all.

No matter what he insisted.

According to those freelance geologists I hired off Craigslist, the hole was a naturally occurring formation that defined a cleft between the outer skin of the Earth and the Hyperborean mantle. The house and ground were unitary that way, sharing a skin, so the cleft led straight down into the planet's core. That's where all the toothpaste was going, along with whatever other bodily fluids I needed to get rid of.

Hey, there was no time for the bathroom if I constantly manned the toothpaste, now was there?

I only hoped I didn't lose the deposit on the room. I hadn't checked whether or not such an activity was prohibited in the establishment's brochure. I doubted management penalized scientific curiosity, but one never knew.

Galileo once had a bad run-in with the exact same sort of thing.

Deliberately Missing Henry Kissinger

I'd always had a thing with heights, but I never thought I'd be afraid of coming down. It seems a bit silly, but strange things can develop when one is on a Ferris wheel and realizes Henry Kissinger is waiting on the ground when there isn't a good explanation for what happened to his 87 Chevy convertible.

The event was difficult to foresee, given that Kissinger didn't usually go in for Scotchtoberfest. It used to be Septemberfest, but no one could remember what the heck that was and a Simpsons homage seemed the right way to go. Even the Ferris wheel cars had been turned into haggis tins rotating around a giant bagpipe.

The noise was awful.

But still, I refused to come down and face Henry. At least, not until I'd come up with a good story about the car. *It's Reagan's fault* was not going to work again, so I kept yelling "Send it around again!" and the carney kept doing that because it was the only English he understood anymore. That's what the city gets for letting traffic court fines be paid in donated brain tissue.

Honestly, who wouldn't see that coming?

Henry hoped to starve me out, but I managed to talk a roving crew of goth street acrobats into regularly bringing me a supply of funnel cakes and deep-fried Twinkies. It wasn't as if I could eat the haggis, though it was cool that they actually filled the tins for authenticity. Good thing I'd sprung for the full version of Acrobat so the crew recognized me as their part-time king. Henry only had the free reader so they wouldn't even talk to him.

Of course, it's not as if there weren't problems in refusing to come down. The Fest only ran for a week each year, so I ended up not existing the rest of the time. I would disappear when it was over and pop into being again the next time. I'm aging wonderfully though, and Henry will have to tire eventually.

I'm definitely glad I got that endless ride pass though. The Ferris wheel would have bankrupted me long ago otherwise.

Ten Gallon Hats Full of Cottage Cheese and the Grassroots Movement to Free K

Dear Doctor Kellogg: please free K. I know you think he is *Special* and all, but that does not justify thirty years solitary confinement. Freeze-dried strawberries are not company. You are cruel and inhumane. There is simply no legitimate excuse for your actions.

Yes, I am aware of the atrocities K committed during the cereal wars of the fifties. Count Chocula's torture using novelty cheese hats, the mass graves in The Land of Half, none of that is a secret. But, what about all the Soggies Cap'n Crunch gassed in the breakfast camps? That dude is still running around free, in command of a vessel no less, so why can't K be free? Sure, that's Quaker and not you, but still.

Besides, how much diabetes did the Count cause, or even the denizens of The Land of Half? It's not as if their hands were completely clean.

The rest of K's treatment is appalling as well. I mean, allowing Guy Fieri to blast K with a fire hose until he went limp enough to be pulled through the cell bars? You call that appropriate procedures for a cell extraction? Guy certainly doesn't. He calls it "taking a trip to Flavortown" when he talks about it down at the eastside Pamida, and he talks about it a lot.

No one disagrees that any use of the term "Flavortown" violates at least nine separate clauses of the Geneva Convention.

We won't even mention vivisection, or the constant diet of uncooked pork and taters flavored Hot Pockets or the fact that you only have extended basic cable on the TV. We all know that's all punishment rather than ordinary prison conditions. It's exactly what you did to Mary Lou Retton.

But don't take my word for it, Amnesty International has taken K's cause up and letters will be rolling in. Free K or you'll get a lot more mail than you're used to getting. Could you handle that? Pretty big threat, isn't it?

Darn right it is.

Sternly yours,

The Alpha-Bits Wizard

Mao Zedong Hid His Metric Spanner in the Potato Salad

It was pretty hot this year at my family's Independence from Belgium Day picnic and all-night celebrity dance-a-thon. Early July in Nebraska is like that, especially with all the tire fires. The celebration was still a good one — toxic fumes notwithstanding.

Few people know about the holiday, being on the fifth right after America's big day. After all, the nation had never been subservient to Belgium the way it had been to England, so the day wasn't really important. Still, after declaring the main independence the founding fathers got really drunk and decided to declare separation from Belgium too. Flip them a gigantic and totally unnecessary bird. No one really cared anymore about such a highly symbolic rude gesture, but my family always observed it since we all worked in the critical sheep appendix repair industry and could never get the fourth off.

Made for some pretty wild times.

I mean, we always had the traditional foods of mouthwash-boiled radishes and creamed Pop Rocks Okra, even blended custard chicken gizzard and rare pork pie. None of us could stomach any of that garbage, but we had it anyway. Just set it all out on the lawn chairs and then snuck out to McDonald's when we actually got hungry. Waterworks shows instead of fireworks, taking big slugs of Monster low-octane Thunderbird -flavored energy drink and spitting at passing taxis, all the usual stuff.

There was that one year that it got us all indicted for treason when one of the taxis was carrying Little Richard on his way to a cell phone battery amnesty summit with Guillermo González Camarena, but you have to expect a rocky Independence from Belgium Day once in a while. It wasn't as if it was an easy day for the founding fathers either, certainly not once the alcohol and

Pitocin poisoning set in.

It should be no surprise that July sixth is the even less remembered I'll Never Drink or Abuse Non-Recreational Obstetric Drugs Again National Day of Observance.

This year went off without a hitch, however. The witnesses weren't able to get a good look at our actual faces due to the rubber Mary Worth masks we wore on our navels and reasonable doubt has become flexible since politeness placed reasonableness in a very personal and context-dependent framework. I do feel sorry for Ann Coulter, but I'm certain her back hair will grow back soon naturally in any event.

Getting to see all the family again made suffering that heat worth it. It'd still be easier if we dispensed with the customary Sumo suit disguises next year. I bet the holiday would feel just as festive without.

Continental Breakfasts Sound Fancy so You Don't Realize It's a God Damned Muffin and You Should Have Just Gone to Tim Hortons

I was never big on Motel 6 or those other cheap, crappy chains…until I learned they could be used to teleport all over the country rather than having to drive. Why else would I stay at one? Frankly, you'd think they'd advertise that part a bit more.

Werner Herzog was the one who finally told me, gave me the low down while we were babysitting Emmanuel Lewis at a Chuck E. Cheese's in Akron. The word "motel" was derived from "motor lodge," Werner said because the damn things were mobile, at least on the ethereal plane. Put the free facial soap in the safe and then hit the desired zip code. The whole building would switch places with the target location and you could walk right out. What did I think those safes were for?

After all, no one at a Motel 6 had money or other valuables to steal, and the safes were easier to remove than the remotes bolted to the nightstand anyway.

I felt somewhat foolish, for not having known…but not as bad as Dwight D. Eisenhower. That little interstate system Ike deployed was a colossal waste of time since we could all just use the motels to teleport.

I wonder why Werner never told him. Dude must have been a Democrat.

The Philosophical Problem of Original Jam

I woke up with strawberry jam smeared in my boxers. I had to say, it was a surprise. It'd never happened before and I'd always thought of myself as a good person.

I mean, I always put a five in the collection plate Sundays for orphans in Beverly Hills. Thus, it couldn't have been karma, or the divine retribution of Fatty Arbuckle.

But it was disconcerting. The jam was smeared around all in there like wallpaper paste in the Nebraska state capital.

When it happened the next night, I went to see a doctor. Figured maybe it was glandular, secretions of fruit sweet jelly ducts, or maybe early-onset male menopause from reading too much Steinbeck in the tub. The doc disagreed, though. Said it was psychosomatic trauma, too much yin in my Oedipal complex ego fuse combined with imbalanced rotation in my collective unconscious capacitor, even though I'd brought in the jam as a sample, which he refused to test any way other than orally.

It appeared again, despite the heavy meds, so I saw a lawyer who shared an office with a furniture dentist and three pet psychics to see if she couldn't enjoin the jam. I thought maybe she'd issue a writ or other order, full of Latin and onions, to keep it a hundred yards away from me.

But she had other plans and dreams, ones of silver yachts and high-priced crackers, and I left with seven articles of incorporation (all duly notarized) and a well-reasoned opinion that declared my right to teach monkeys French.

Meanwhile, this was costing money, hundreds in soiled boxers alone. Cash was tight too, tied up in Swiss Franc futures and cold baked beans.

So I started wearing toast boxers to bed, Oroweat to be precise. I had breakfast whenever I woke, just to clean things up. Sides of sliced Brie. And it all worked out, in a way. Though, I really preferred Cream of Wheat and a muffin.

The Barometric Pressure of Hickory-Smoked Country Ham

Man, I wish I had a job as the specials forecaster at the Cracker Barrel. Those guys can be wrong at least half the time and no one even bats an eye. Meanwhile, us line cooks get fired for anything approaching those kind of stats, and that's not even considering the rare case where someone's flooded out of their summer home as a result.

Last Tuesday, perfect example. The server said there was a 90% chance that Uncle Herschel's Favorite® was the special. That internet trick for reducing arterial plaque using a corkscrew everyone's been talking about was working great, so I went for it. Unfortunately, my breakfast came out as the pickled severed heads of the Bee Gees, though still with that side of the hash brown casserole.

Of course, the severed heads of the Bee Gees had been fugitives from The Hague due to war crimes for six generations. I was immediately arrested by the Swiss Guard and summarily executed by Nerf firing squad. I tell you, if it wasn't for the fact that the Swiss Guard don't work for The Hague, I might really have been in trouble.

The execution might have counted then and I would have been at least a little dead. I can thank Oliver North and Emmanuel Goldstein for that loophole.

Still, I had to give up my Western way of life in favor of hydroponically growing Cream of Wheat in an industrial sector of Southern Namibia. I mean, what other choice did I have after those heads? I certainly wasn't going to be finishing breakfast, not with all that lame singing, and there weren't a whole lot of other options given my limited food-based skill set.

If only I'd trained at home for a better career as a space monkey paleontologist instead of choosing the free microwave.

The server was no help at all. She simply explained that on 90% of days historically with similar conditions, the special had been Uncle Herschel's Favorite®. There were complicating factors that could muddle things though, such as the stock price of the Digital Equipment Corporation in late March of 1982 or the number of movies where Jim Varney had been secretly replaced with a dyslexic orangutan, and nothing was guaranteed.

Severed heads of the Bee Gees just sometimes happened… though perhaps they would clear soon.

Mind you, we had that conversation over Aldis lamp semaphore transmissions from Namibia. It wasn't as if I could leave the Cream of Wheat lab for long, and the landline wouldn't be installed until the next week. Even then, only if I remembered to stir regularly.

The Namibian government was notoriously unforgiving about lumpy Cream of Wheat.

The Federal Reserve Isn't Any Safer if You Get Called Up to Active Duty

If people don't take time to find outlets for their creativity, it's just going to pop out *somewhere*. Alan Greenspan is a perfect example, even if he is in jail now. That's what trespassing and vandalism charges will get you though, even with his kind of connections.

I'd thought the supply room simply hadn't been cleaned in a long time. That wasn't particularly important after all since no clients ever saw it. Who cared if there were unexplained stains on the wall? Ketchup? Coffee? Soda? There was no real way to say, but they were there. No real way to know where they'd come from either since we never stored food in there. It was only used for copy paper.

So, what the heck, I sent our attorney to wipe down the walls in there. He's on retainer anyway, so what was the harm?

But the stains came back the next day, exactly as before. That's when I set the bear trap…lined with Nerf from old footballs of course, since I didn't want another lawsuit. I figured I'd catch some of the furniture elves that hide in the acoustic ceiling tiles, or Harvey Keitel again, but I have to say I was shocked to find Alan Greenspan stuck there when I came in the following morning.

Seriously, I hadn't even realized he'd come back from his semester abroad studying nuclear botany in Puyallup.

Turns out, Alan was *painting* back there. Murals all titled "Mysterious Stains," subtitled variation one through eight hundred and thirty-seven. Really, he was simply smearing whatever crap he happened to have on our walls. Don't say that to him though, he's quite sensitive about it.

Artists can be so delicate about their work.

Calling the cops was about the only way to end it. Either that, or we'd have had to come up with nice things to say to Alan about his use of color. We certainly weren't going to do that, and couldn't think of anything anyway.

We mostly went in for impressionists as purely a matter of personal taste.

1788 Botany Bay was a Poor Choice for a Fundamentalist Family Vacation

Tooth care has gotten so complicated these days, now that smart phones are everywhere. I blame the Australians; frankly, I think they're conning me. First, it was only brushing and flossing, and you only had to do it twice a day and after meals, but then there were water picks, extra fluoride treatments, and interdental flosser brushes that look like repurposed pipe cleaners. When the Australians came, it only got worse.

I had weak teeth anyway due to that acetone gargling habit, so I went to see Paul Hogan. He still dressed as Crocodile Dundee and was going to pick tartar off my teeth with that big Bowie knife of his. You know, like those little birds do for alligators in the cartoons at the dentist's office. He said I needed more though, needed to coat each tooth in luxury-level clear nail polish each morning before facing the day. Only then would I be protected against the acid rain mist that was everywhere in the air, and gritting my teeth in traffic all the time. That is, if I wanted to avoid dentures by fifty.

Of course, I also had to grind it all off at night using coarse-grit diamond sanding pads before I went to bed. Left on, the nocturnal chemical reaction with the enamel would only make my teeth worse.

But that abrading hurt, so I ended up going to Jacko so he could "Oi!" my teeth into submission, menacing them with a pack of AA Energizer batteries. I thought his treatment might surprise me, though I wasn't prepared for unconventional therapies such as eucalyptus/Koala-based new wave mesmerism. He was the one who convinced me to encapsulate everything I ate and drank in platinum-coated industrial contact adhesive to completely isolate it all from my teeth, but it's also possible he was kidding. Australian humor is hard to understand, and it didn't keep me from needing to go to Men at Work next.

Side note, a Vegemite sandwich does NOTHING good for your teeth.

The expenses were really piling up, but how could I say no? Wasn't proper dentition worth it to me? What was all the money for high-end nail polish, sandpaper, contact adhesive, and Wonder Bread compared to my oral health? I was afraid to be skeptical.

I drew the line, though, at armoring each tooth with old cans of Foster's. I'm not sure if Olivia Newton-John even counts as Australian for dental purposes anyway.

One does have to remain vigilant.

Butter Has Not Been Approved by the FDA as a Low-Calorie Food Substitute Because That Stuff is Fattening as Hell, Dawg

Note to self: the explorer primarily responsible for initiating the wave of European colonialism into the New World was not Bozo the Clown. It was also not Wizzo. I have no idea where Clarence got that information, but it was completely inaccurate, so much so that I was given detention and a wild badger. I cannot ignore my suspicions that this was not a mistake on Clarence's part, that this misinformation was a deliberate act to destroy my academic good name. "Dealing with Clarence" should be added to my upcoming to-do agenda.

Note to self: paying Courtney Love free McDonald's cheeseburger coupons to kill Clarence may not have been the best idea. Apparently, Courtney thinks getting torn to shreds bare-handedly by a drug-addled and shrieking grunge-rock celebrity is an accident. The fact it was as Clarence was successfully answering the last question of the International Spelling Bee and Guess the Number I'm Thinking of finals didn't help, particularly since Courtney was my date to that event. I really should have at least asked if she even cared what the definition of "accident" was. I don't think she did.

Note to Self: Hi, Will! I enjoyed *The Quantity Theory of Insanity* very much. That has absolutely nothing to do with my problems regarding Courtney and Clarence, but I had some time while I was figuring out what to do about them and I figured I'd get this out of the way.

Note to self: "My bad" is no longer a perfect defense to a murder conspiracy charge in the lower forty-eight contiguous and low-fat United States processed cheese foods. Word remains out on Alaska and Serutan, but the Borax Reclassification and Rehabilitation Act of 1997 appears to have altered the landscape of legal defenses to violent crimes, as well as adjusting acceptable weights for medical-grade carp, in response to that whole "Sinbad starred in *Shazam*" thing. I might want to get another attorney.

Note to self: it was a stroke of pure luck that the judge had also recently bought test answers off Clarence. I wasn't going to tell him what had actually happened, but he said "pretty please" and then dismissed all the charges once he knew the full story. As it happened, he also hired Courtney Love to kill Clarence and we had no way of knowing which of us was co-conspirator to the actual murder. Reasonable doubt, baby. Reasonable doubt.

Note to self: why am I even writing these? I don't ever read them later. I could have probably used the time to study and not ever had to pay Clarence for test answers in the first place. That would have saved time. Oh well, live and learn… or not, in Clarence's case.

It's Really Hard to Hide Flapjacks in Your Pockets When Flying Frontier

They finally lost my Polaroid off the wall of people permanently banned from the premises for nudity and health code violations, so I ended up at Village Inn for brunch this weekend. Ordered a veggie omelet with a side of crispy bacon because I'm still not fully committed to the vegetarian lifestyle yet, and I like confusing servers. Mine didn't seem to care but was otherwise nervous. Maybe she remembered me from that previous Icy Hot incident.

It was cool though, except when she brought me pie. I mean in my omelet.

Seriously, the omelet was a French silk pie base with chunks of lemon meringue pie, cherry pie, and key lime pie scatted throughout. Blended up and fried with coconut cream pie butter, garnished with shaved banana cream pie like it was mozzarella cheese. Even the bacon was southern pecan pie, stretched and pounded out flat before being cooked to a crisp. My soda was caramel apple pie a la mode.

"What gives?" I asked my waitress, though she was hesitant about approaching my table. "What's with all the pie?"

They'd gone gung-ho with the pie, she informed me. Committed to it heavy. Lots of people came for the pie, and it used to simply be that they'd offer it at the end of every meal, even when someone stopped in for only coffee. Then there was Free Pie Wednesday, a push to increase pie sales since they kept saying the pie was free but most kinds people wanted, not simple fruit varieties, didn't qualify. Then they said to hell with it and did this.

Apparently, Rupert Murdoch had finally gone completely nuts, had a bad reaction to a mix of cocaine and powdered Drano. Decided pie wasn't a choice anymore, instead a requirement. Replaced pie for every ingredient in the menu.

Pancakes? Pie. Waffles? Pie. Eggs? Pie.

You get the idea.

He also whacked Bronson Pinchot. The whole deal was pretty wild, especially since Rupert didn't even own Village Inn. What could they do though?

Honestly, after Bronson they probably worried they might be next.

I dug pie as much as the next person, even considering that Rob Reiner was in the adjacent booth, but this was a bit much for me. I'd developed type six diabetes already and I hadn't even gotten to dessert. Good thing I was planning on getting kicked out for life again anyway.

I'm not sure how much more I could have taken.

Socrates Didn't Fill Out His School Permission Slip for the Senate Trip Completely so Octavian Made Him Stay Behind and Work the Counter at a Chain of Gynaeceum Gift Shops Instead

I'd planned to follow the Dead that summer when I was seven, but the tires on the family station wagon needed to be re-vulcanized so I had to hang around Greece while my parents rebuilt the Acropolis so we could get money for that. Socialist forces in the Italian government sold the whole thing at auction while they were drunk and needed to make sure their dad didn't notice when he got home.

Fun fact: seventy-five percent of high-schooler groundings in Europe are related to sales of the Acropolis when intoxicated, the majority of which are attributable to Four Loko alone. The other twenty-five percent are a hodgepodge of fine art theft, hobo murder, and exportation of the tags off of mattresses without filing the proper declarations. It's true.

Anyway, so that's how I spent my school break that year.

You'd think I'd have learned something about ancient history and culture or whatnot, but my parents didn't have a lot of room doing the job. Italy is a pretty strict taskmaster, all business, and no fun. Just ask Isabella Rossellini; she'll tell you any day.

Presuming she's not giving you the silent treatment again.

I mainly spent my time cataloging the human genome according to the Dewey Decimal System. That didn't even take long since I cataloged the whole thing as one entry, and under "H" no less since I wasn't real up on Dewey, getting the World Scientific Ethical Board all over my case anyway. Something about playing Goddard, but who cared?

I was only killing time.

Life improved once the job was done and my parents could return to Detroit. We weren't from there, but I guess we didn't read our plane tickets real close so it was to Detroit that we went. Now Detroit was some living, and let me tell you… those tires had never been so vulcanized.

It was like magic, the kind of magic that only happens when you're seven…or overcome by asphalt fumes.

The Belated Introduction of Encumbrance Tables in the Original Chutes and Ladders Board Game Crushed Many Players When They Reached Level Four

I'm not the reason that there are hobbits in my apartment. I keep my place clean, but that's the problem with communal living. It's cheap, and the agents of Alexander Hamilton have a great deal more trouble secretly abducting you in the middle of the night in order to learn your bowling secrets, but you can get hobbits.

All it takes is one neighbor who digs fantasy shtick. Maybe they read old pulp paperbacks to Barbara Bush on the weekends. Perhaps they host *Buckaroo Banzai Goes to Washington* fan club meetings. They might even run games of Dungeons & Donner Parties, but the exact specifics don't really matter. The next thing you know, the whole building is spilling over with hobbits.

The first time it happens, people always try to use cheap poison traps or spray cans from the supermarket…but those don't do much of anything. No one ever believes that if you tell them though. People can't imagine the FDA would let them in stores if they didn't do *something*. Heck, even I'm not sure why Roxy Carmichael lets the pest control companies get away with that, but they certainly won't rid you of hobbits. Unless they're really just short film extras trying to scam a free place to crash until the midterm elections, you're still going to have groups trying to destroy the One Ring again in just a few days.

Sure, the bombs at least kill a few. Who wouldn't think they work when you find dead hobbits all over your kitchen floor? However, hobbits crawl into walls through electrical socket plates. The gas simply can't reach far enough and they'll breed double hard to make up the difference. Unless you can bomb within the walls as well as without, you're really best off calling a hobbit removal specialist who is licensed to use the heat treatment instead of poison.

I mean, it isn't common knowledge, but hobbits can't have breakfast if the ambient temperature is above a hundred and ten degrees Fahrenheit. It curdles the clotted cream which hobbits refuse to breakfast without. They starve within hours, mainly due to their genetic predisposition toward hypoglycemia. The best removal outfits use dragon turbines for the heat generation, which works a heck of a lot better than that Tolkien propaganda would have you believe. Just trust me if you want the buggers gone quickly.

Try explaining all that to my eHarmony date though. There's nothing more embarrassing than starting to make out on the couch only to discover you're sitting in the middle of a shire. She ran out faster than I could say "Joe's Apartment," which is something I was not likely to say no matter how long she gave me.

After all, it's just a goddamned figure of speech.

Everything is Funny if You're Drunk Enough, Mom

Perky people aerobic dancing in blue and red leotards invaded the planet and it was too damn early for any of us to deal with their crap. Honestly, perky first thing in the morning? That was triable as a war crime in virtually any correspondence VCR repair school moot court competition in the country. Maybe even the world.

The perky people aerobic dancing in blue and red leotards took us pretty much by surprise. They landed in day-glow flying saucers made of taped-together paper plates from last Sunday's church picnic in Grand Island covered with military grade aluminum foil, dull side out. That's how they fooled our radar early-warning-perky people detection systems, that and the fact that the radar operators didn't get up until noon.

It was probably a mistake conceding that point in the union talks.

The army had no weapon that worked on the perky people aerobic dancing in blue and red leotards. They tried generic supermarket soda pop, deflated basketball hoops that were pulling out of the garage wall to darn near the point of falling off, and even the *CBS Storybreak* (caffeinated and regular). They had to get all the leaders of the world to turn their skate keys at the same time in the Ballard Locks to launch the last one, being the ultimate doomsday weapon and all, but all to no noticeable effect.

The perky people aerobic dancing in blue and red leotards simply kept coming, and dancing.

Buckminster Fuller warned us this could happen, used the psychic powers he developed studying at the DeVry Institute when that Edelbrock Performance Carburetor fell on his head, but we didn't listen. Why would we? Who'd believe him about perky people aerobic dancing in blue and red leotards? No one even paid attention after he was wrong about it for the first eight times.

Damn sneaky perky people aerobic dancing in blue and red leotards.

The worst part was their haircuts. The men were the worst, but the women were almost as bad. Were those late seventies styles or eighties? No one could really tell for sure, and it was driving us all nuts. Top scientists were working round the clock on the issue, organized by experts in the field such as LL Cool J and Madeleine Albright.

Most of us were simply ignoring the perky people aerobic dancing in blue and red leotards for the moment. Despite the invasion, they didn't seem to be doing a whole lot other than that freaky aerobic dancing while that crappy schmaltz song played. Maybe we'd do something about them once we woke up a little.

We had to get some coffee in us first.

I was Never Big on Lamentations Because Citrus Gives me Gas

We'd always assumed "Then God blessed the seventh day and made it holy, because on it he rested from all the work of creating that he'd done" referred to Sunday, so we were surprised to find out it meant a run-down bar outside Flint, Michigan. Biblical scholars at the Pearl Buck Institute of Cream Cheese and Herpes Lesions confirmed it though, the phrase referred to The Seventh Day Bar & Grill, a bit of a dive but a good place never the less. Apparently, the Lord felt he needed a cold one after his long first week and picked that particular establishment to hang out atop while quaffing a brew.

Happened to mess up the roof real good.

Once everyone learned the bar was holy, on word of no less than the Lord himself, no one dared charge them any taxes. Religious exemption. No liquor tax, sales tax, property tax, or Mexican-Armenian War Retraction and American Idol Voting Poll Tax. Nothing.

That bar had it made.

Other people got into the act as well. You started seeing "God slept here" signs pop up all over the East Coast, tax exemption claim filed accordingly since the places must therefore also be holy by the same rationale. They sold the placards at Walmart of all places, right next to the hybrid nuclear reactor conversion kits and pre-chewed Toll House chocolate chip cookies. That's how common they were. No one wanted to pay taxes of any kind, ad valorem in particular.

The relevant authorities weren't sure what to do, both civil and ecclesiastic. Shoe salesmen had a hell of a time since so many had to go barefoot, the ground upon which almost everyone walked purportedly being hallowed.

People claimed God slept in their paychecks, that he napped on their poker winnings. There was even talk of granting God a disability pension for narcolepsy, seeing as he was having such a tough time staying awake.

God the all-sleeping, as he came to be known.

Most governments would have gone bankrupt if someone hadn't thought to charge a God occupancy tax, no religious exemption allowed. It might have created a bit of a furor, but I think everyone was sick of the whole thing by then. Besides, most people were more immediately concerned then with trying to settle the new wave of Buddha car crash claims.

There were simply bigger problems at hand.

The Prime Directive by Definition Isn't Evenly Divisible by Either Dried Strawberries or Opie Taylor

I thought the gravel on the side of my house was normal until that night I saw Gene Roddenberry out there loading some up in a *Bob the Builder* wheelbarrow. My first thought was to confront him, but he was gone too quick. Old Gene has gotten fast since he started hawking that holographic yogurt-based home ankle fitness rubber band system.

Faster than me, at least.

I kept seeing him out there, always late at night when I was watching old episodes of *Sanford and Son Meet the Cannibal Tribes of Indonesia*. Always dressed in denim overalls with no shirt…Gene not me. I was in my reflective nylon tuxedo, as one might expect. I'm not a savage, after all.

Finally, I got curious and started digging around out there. Did you know that gravel went down well over ten feet without hitting actual dirt? It looked like a lot more, but any deeper and it kept caving in on my head as I dug.

That stung a little.

What really stopped me though was Rex Harrison showing up and saying I'd be arrested by federal marshals if I didn't cease. Apparently, my house was located on the National Gravel Mine Reserve, the source for all gravel in the country. It went straight down to the Earth's core and bubbled up to the surface, but only Gene Roddenberry had the license to mine it…won that in a game of Crazy Eights with Madeleine Albright and Larry Flynt back when he was head of General Mills. Anybody else would get locked up faster than car doors during a Sunday afternoon drive through Shawnee Mission, Kansas.

Wish he'd told me that before arresting me though. Federal prison put a bit of a damper on my evening.

Still, it was kind of an ego boost to have my house located on a spot that critical to the development of our country. I mean, movie production would grind to a halt without a steady supply of gravel for all those addicted Hollywood types, given that mainstream movies now make up 80% of our GNP since the Federal Bureau of Furniture and Non-Futon Bedding recalled most varieties of cheddar spray cheese. It gave me some street cred on CellBlock D, though not quite enough to quality for double commissary points.

You've got to be a real high roller to get that.

Polident Commercials for Indentured Servitude

My cat asked to switch places with me this morning, and that concerned me for a number of reasons. Foremost was the fact that non-speech was an essential and non-severable term of his hiring agreement. That breach alone justified immediate termination and total loss of 401K. Also, he said it in Dutch and he knows that pisses me off.

Still, it was the anniversary of the day Emmanuel Lewis sailed from Spain in the 1700s to discover banana pudding buried in Greenwich Village. I had to let things slide in the spirit of the holidays.

Besides, I liked the idea of getting a break from work.

So, he went off that morning instead of me. Got himself dressed all up in a full suit complete with collar stays and bifurcated gallium-tin shirt cuffs. Looked very professional, I must say. That was weird too though, given that I work as the nighttime door checker at an underground Baskin Robbins fight club franchise.

His mistake, right? Being overdressed was the least of his problems when the lactose intolerance riots started, and I had some serious relaxation to get into. Maybe even convert my crotch to microfiche.

I suppose I should have double-checked what he actually did all day. I thought I knew, but remember that old chestnut about assumptions making a marmalade omelet out of nineteenth-century Athenian fur trappers? One could get a wicked surprise. I mean, I didn't even know there was a SweeTARTS mine under the house; much less that he was the main cart pusher down there.

Having Ernest Borgnine as a foreman didn't help either. Who even knew that guy was still around?

Seriously, that was some hard work. Even with pretending to be dead for four hours due to Romex fire fumes, it was the hardest day I'd ever had. That raw SweeTARTS dust starts to burn when it mixes with your sweat, and that was even before the cave-in trapped me with Lady Bird Johnson and she chewed through my appendix before we were freed.

Tough.

It gave me a whole new appreciation for that cat, let me tell you. I only hoped he came back soon. I was a little concerned once I realized he took all his stuff with him when he left.

Turns Out The Pizza Hut BOOK IT! Program Was Not for Fleeing Tax Evasion Charges

The other kids were all suckers. EVERYBODY had a lemonade stand, even that Russian guy down the street who mainly talked to Latvian men in Oscar Mayer Wienermobiles about "targets" and didn't seem interested in selling any actual lemonade. I was the only entrepreneur with enough vision to sell cake door-to-door.

Who could say no to cake? When it showed up on its own? I made a mint! Mint chocolate, but still.

Sure, there were a few logistical issues in the beginning, such as supply. One tray of cake wasn't cost effective. That's eight pieces? Ten? I barely got down the block. I needed to have more at a time, far more.

That's when I got that plastic five-gallon paint bucket.

You might not think people would want a handful of cake that's just been jammed into a giant plastic bucket by a ten-year-old with serious sinus allergy problems, but you'd be as wrong as Johannes Kepler about the Pog fad. It's not as if I didn't wash my hands, use of their sink and soap simply being part of the purchase price, so everyone was good. Even the health department checked off, though they were strangely more concerned with how much toffee bits were in my cake, per slice.

I think someone misread their job duties.

Anyway, I was a huge success. Soon I had to expand, mentally divide myself and astrally project several times a day in order to meet door-to-door cake requests as far away as the Bastille Day crowds outside the Boll Weevil Monument in Enterprise, Alabama. Admittedly, I had to kill that sumo wrestler outside Dayton who went around offering people free bites from his coconut raspberry Zingers, but that was all part of doing business.

Even Marie Antoinette, the chick who washed motorcycle windows outside the organic rubber galoshes co-op for buffalo nickels and an occasional cobb salad, would tell you that. It was business, man.

Cake business.

90% of All Sourdough Turtles Break Apart in the Water on Their Very First Trip to the Sea

Garth Algar really ruins a trip to the *Ripley's Believe It or Not!* museum. You remember…the sidekick guy from *Wayne's World*? He kept following me around as I looked at exhibits, trying to decide whether I believed or not, and loudly asserting the latter.

And it was supposed to be the highlight of my annual National Pickle Week vacation to the San Francisco waterfront.

The honest congressman from Borneo? "Not!" The tomato a Michigan househusband grew as big as a pumpkin that also looked exactly like a pumpkin and was made out of pumpkin? "Not!" The volleyball-sized sweat ruby bearing a mysterious curse causing whoever came into possession of it to pay a substantial and expensive luxury tax? "Not!"

It was pretty annoying, honestly. I can see why the guy hadn't worked since the films, that and only being a character instead of an actual person. Museum staff kept suggesting I leave so he'd go too, but they stopped short of actually deigning to speak to him about the problem.

His kind of negativity spoiled the whole intent of that sort of museum. People went there for curiosity, sure. However, it was the ambiguous state that was the real draw. Like Denny's. The exhibits were so fantastic…you couldn't quite believe…but it was all true. Well, true more or less. They stretched a few things… such as Nixon's high score on PAC-MAN. Agnew might have played a couple levels while Tricky was in the bathroom. Still, you get the idea. You get how Garth's skepticism killed the mood.

So…you understand what I had to do.

And that's the truth. I realize you asked me why I was carving Steve McQueen's face into the back of the Statue of Liberty's head, but I stand by what I've said…more or less.

Himmler's Hidden Alien Civil War Gold Caused that Detroit Pawnshop Storage Locker to Lose its International Real Estate Flipping License

With as many TV shows and movies as there were about it, I think people were actually hoping for a zombie plague. How else would you explain the obsession? I don't think people were particularly hoping for an invasion of zombie Eva Braun clones, but humanity never has been real careful what it wishes for. Just look at all those turgor pressure themed Saturday morning cartoons.

You all remember Eva though. She was Hitler's girl. That isn't especially relevant to her animated clone corpses eating brains, but what is? Her work to ban bean-flavored Fritos in the former Soviet republics doesn't excuse anything either, whether the parts before or after her original death.

Lucky she turned out to have an unexplained aversion to any Conagra brand of spray cheese. The presence of even a single can turned her right around and had her headed straight back to the sea. Due to the Easy Cheese World Subsidy Initiative of 2013, that meant earth was pretty much safe. Sure, the oceans were full of Evas, but you can't have everything.

Life is full of compromises.

And after all, the sea was partially responsible in the first place. Corroding broadband internet cables under water carrying History Channel Nazi documentaries bled the idea of Eva into the Sargasso algae beds. Given all the pollution down there, it was an eventuality that Eva clones would develop therefrom. They drowned, but the repeated syndication broadcasts reanimated them again. Sooner or later, they'd march to the land looking for brains.

Of course, then they'd go back again because of the spray cheese. It was monotonous, but many coastal nations made fortunes on tollbooths. I guess you can't blame them.

All in all, it probably wasn't the worst thing that could happen. At least the Nazis themselves stayed dead. Then again, considering how much many of them owe Blockbusters for late fees on *Air Bud* rentals, they'd probably hide even if they did rise from the grave.

Just like the rest of us.

Rain Drops on Roses and Beer-Battered Fish Shoved Into Video Rental Return Boxes

Ten days into the conference, I began to wish I'd read the materials I'd seen tattooed on the severed head of Andy Griffith a bit more carefully. After all, the fact it listed an opening date but not a closing one suggested it would go on for eternity. What else would that indicate? I should have noticed. I'd been warned just like I'd been warned not to use my Craftsman lawnmower for internal purposes.

It was my own fault.

That didn't make me feel any better though, sitting in the back of a conference hall scribbling on a hotel stationary notebook while listening to some person up front drone on about bifurcated panel decisions. Honestly, I couldn't even remember what the conference was about anymore. Zoo safety standards? Power plant regulations? Cream cheese consumption statistics? I'm not sure if I ever knew. Maybe no one else did either. Those kind of conferences could kind of start on their own, like Bolivian Marshmallow Flu.

Most of us were still sitting in our chairs, no matter how uncomfortable that might have been on our bedsores. A few brave souls had set up campsites in the hall though, made tents out of broken tables and ripped-up carpet fragments. They even cooked a bellhop over a fire started by rubbing two portable coffee pots together. That was certainly resourceful, though I wasn't sure they were even hungry.

Simply bored.

It seemed as if more of us would join the campers in a day or two. We were certainly looking their way. Maybe we'd all abandon the speaker and form a new society organized around the non-canonical episodes of *Knight Rider* dubbed into Spanish, or emulate the cobbling practices of Imelda Marcos.

But I bet we weren't going to be smart enough to leave… presuming we were even able to.

At least we were going to get credit for it though. No one seemed to know what the credit was, or what it was for, but we knew for sure we were going to get it. We had to get something; surely we deserved it for sacrificing that intern. We definitely wanted it, or we would have left with the British plague rats long before.

We all wanted something or would have been at the Mary Kay convention with Judd Hirsch at the other side of the hotel instead.

Much of What We Think We Know About the Ancient Greek Phrenologists Was Faked as a Joke by Sarcastic Franciscan Monks Who Were Ticked That Isabella Rossellini Wouldn't Let Them Join the Freedent Rebel Alliance

What if Socrates was just really thirsty and said: "Oh well."

It Was Pointless to Work Out THACOs for Standard Cucumber Rolls Because the Things Never Won Initiative Anyway

I found that I could substantially increase the armor class of my day-to-day apparel by rubbing shaving cream into the fabric each morning before Church. That technique provided just a little more protection against stabbing weapons, blades, and even bludgeon-based attacks. Considering I normally wore a T-shirt and jeans, I thought I could use any enhancement I could get…what with all the freelance Mounties that started hanging out downtown by the 7–Elevens.

Barbasol was my preference, but I suppose the brand didn't matter too much. The fact that Julius Caesar was a Gillette man indicated nothing about the suitability of that particular shaving cream. Still, it was hard to ignore the psychological implications, as well as the Plácido Domingo effect.

Especially when dodging blowgun darts in Brooklyn.

I believe it was the stiffness the shaving cream added to the fabric that made the difference. The combination became just that much more difficult to pierce or tear, and even provided a little cushioning. Aristotle wrote an ode to similar properties of ambergris, but shaving cream was pretty similar and certainly was the closest Americans could get since that Eddie Bauer embargo was put into place after the low-rise denim riots back in spring.

We all had to make do with what we had.

Granted, rubbing clothes with any kind of cream made it a tad more difficult to move and one did lose a little flexibility that way, but Elle Macpherson definitively proved that the property of being lubricated when moving through air at any elevation below ten thousand feet more than made up for it.

David Letterman would never have her back after that episode, but his show ended soon thereafter, so who cared?

Certainly not the British secret service, apparently.

But enough about that. To make a long story short, I didn't have to start wearing that Armani full-plate-mail suit to work after all. Penny's was going to give me hell about returning it, but they'd come around eventually once the interstellar lawyers got involved. They'd have to.

It was still within the original ninety days, and I still had the receipt.

My Degree in Topiatrical Surgery Won't Stop Vin Diesel From Repossessing my Spleen

In the future, we'll all live on my genetically modified green bean plantation. It'll be great. The beans will develop gigantic size and sentience so they can serve us, satisfying our every chicken-related whim. We'll tell them we're gods of mayonnaise and they will worship us as the reincarnated holy band of minstrels Haricot Verts, at least until Norman Rockwell spills our secrets under hours and hours of excruciating Richard Marx themed torture.

We will not know why we tortured Norman, or how he came to be alive again. The beans will not have been involved, for the most part being a peaceful chlorophyll-filled race.

The future will be baffling to many.

After that, in the future, we will go begging for used M&M packets in Times Square. We will not be able to use my millions in hydrogen-7 futures to retire to a subterranean aboveground condo in the technological hub that will be the Lesser Antilles because I will have lost every cent in a breakfast pill startup company. Who will have been able to guess that another company would market a gummy version on the exact same day?

Certainly not the cybernetic shadowed hologram of argon-39 George Foreman, sent back in time to rescue the Chilean anti-rebels from the polar bear automotive scientists. He'll be with us, one of the breakfast pill company's largest investors.

Some people are simply bad with money.

The used M&Ms won't be worth much on their own, but we'll glue them together with Post-its to construct a gigantic M&M palace in Little Rock, Arkansas. People will think it's the lost shrine of Marisa Tomei since most of their knowledge of the early twenty-first-century will have been derived from Super 8 Lady Gaga music videos.

Thank God for the song: "Coat my Ass in Bacon and Take me to the Candy-Coated Chocolate Monument to the Goddess of *My Cousin Vinnie*." It will have been a classic.

We'll be treated as gods again, this time of foam pool cleaning equipment, brought AM Walkmans and dusty cans of Diet Pepsi by religious pilgrims coming to worship the past. The claim will be that we'll burn the offerings in secret once they've gone, but how would we pay our protection tithe to the Overchurch of the Black Amex if we did?" Besides, burning plastic will have been made a class thirty-five controlled substance upon discovery that it tended to grant transdermal tooth immortality.

No, we'll be happy with our little roadside monk gig and abuse our powers to get metal chicks. At least, that's what the prophecy will read.

It's hard to be precise.

If That Waitress Sprays Me With the Soda Water One More Time I'm Going to Move to Cedar Rapids and Study TV/VCR Repair With Rod Serling

I can't believe Ron Perlman keeps coming back to our bar after all the times we've kicked his ass. Seriously, it seems as if we've just pulled out his toenails with a three-hole staple punch before putting him in a taxi bound for Disneyland Paris and going inside to order another beer when his gravely voice comes from that same corner booth, speculating that Hostess uses Miracle Whip to get Suzy Q's to stay chewy in milk. What's up with that?

At first, he sat there quietly sipping Goldschläger martinis. Then he started saying things though, things that guaranteed we'd come after him, things about all-American snack food.

"Tyson thinks about the devil while roasting pepper variety Ball Park Jerky." "Everlasting Gobstoppers figured heavily into most naval battles of the Crimean War." "Dole pineapples were created in a laboratory by hybrid semantic constructs of Marie Curie and Leon Trotsky."

He had to be *trying* to piss us off.

I mean, this was a workingman's bar. Most of us whipped corset-wearing pigs with limp garlic spaghetti noodles over at the Kellogg's plant for a living. We didn't want to hear any of that pinko snack conspiracy garbage about the holy United States food industry. None of us would take that crap from the *Sports Illustrated* swimsuit model fitness videos, so why would we put up with it from him?

Hellboy was *not* that great a movie.

So, we kept going round. Took out his kidneys with olive

oil greased saps and made him vote *Ishtar* for best picture, sent him to California to make bacon Brussels sprout casserole, coated him in oxblood shoe polish and took his picture for our passports…we did it all. No matter what we did though, that fucker kept coming right back.

Maybe he was only trying to get out of having to pay for his drinks. I could totally see that.

I'm Going to Lick the Envelope Flap in Morse Code to Signal for Help

No, I can't go to the all-you-can-eat-chicken-and-waffles-square-dance event at the state capital building interrogation room this morning. I need to work on my entry for the Publisher's Clearing House Sweepstakes instead before Lance Armstrong beats me out again. I bet you people didn't even know they still sent those envelopes out anymore, thought they'd shutdown after the underground postal revolution of 1972, but I got one this year. That's what comes from joining the hemorrhoid sufferer of the month club and getting on the really good mailing lists.

I may already be a winner, but only if I can figure out which of my internal organs they've hidden the little stamps in that I need to cut out and paste on the Teflon aluminum coated microfiche form. I bet it's my appendix. No one ever thinks to look there. Those things are so tricky since they started making the stamps out of flesh and don't print them with any ink.

Not everyone has what it takes for this.

Of course, you don't have to buy any magazines…but isn't it a coincidence that the last winner was found crushed to death under the immense mountains of *Redbook* and *Woman's Day* that almost entirely filled his five-bedroom, seventy-three bathroom prefabricated vinyl home? Somehow the winners just seem to be people like that. Too bad he was already dead when the prize van rolled up with their cameras and Christian Scientist civil war relocation personnel.

Made for somewhat of a downer of a commercial.

Still, the main entry wouldn't take up my entire day… but what about the other prizes I could win hidden in the advertisements stuffing that envelope? All I have to do to win a refurbished '87 Citation station wagon complete with 53-inch Zenith wood paneled console television is to write a dissertation on micro-financing at ShowBiz Pizza and complete the course hours for my Ph.D. There's also a lifetime supply of abalone flavored butterscotch pudding for the person who most accurately guesses Ed McMahon's blood sugar at the time of his death without going over.

All kinds of things interspersed, reverse Manchester encoded, in those circulars for publications like *Swank* and *Highlights for Children*.

So no. No socializing for me today. I'm going to be ready for that prize van, along with any Belgian mercenaries they bring along. Maybe this time I won't be ruled ineligible because of that pro-crop pollination subversive discussion group and Scholastic science fiction book club I joined at the library during middle school.

Do we never get forgiven for the mistakes of our youth?

Keebler Elves Live in Hollow Trees and Can Really Gum Up a Chainsaw

I found a vast and complex miniature civilization of tiny elves living in the cardboard cylinder of my Quaker Oats that I had hidden for years in the back of my pantry behind the pumpkin filling cans and the sugar-frosted lentils. They were delicious, flavored like little corn syrup-colored berries. I didn't even need to use honey. Considering their body fat content, I didn't need to use butter either.

They were so cute, all dressed in elegantly somber black jackets and wide-brimmed hats. It looked like something right out of the eighteen-hundreds, except done in dusty oatmeal. Well…I guess that's right out of the eighteen-hundreds too. We just don't think of it that way modernly due to the influence of the Kellogg's Mafia. Corn Flakes are revisionist history.

I caught them in the process of raising a barn. At least, I think it was a barn. It's hard to tell when the building materials are dry-carburetor ground oats. Just ask Frank Lloyd Wright. There were tiny horses being stored there though, so I guessed barn. I doubted they were animals enough to store horses in an abattoir.

They addressed me quite politely. It was all "thees" and "thous." The politeness remained even as I began cooking and consuming them, only becoming slightly more stern. I believe a "Lord" of some kind may have been invoked. Frankly, I might have eaten them at that point simply to stop the noise.

I've never been much for Dickens.

Whatever Bobcat Goldthwait tells you otherwise is a lie.

I didn't see how they didn't expect I would eat them. I mean, they were in my oatmeal. The fact that I hadn't touched it for decades was utterly beside the point, no matter what they said. I was certainly going to have some that morning, and I wasn't awake enough at that moment to wait. There was no adverse possession of uncooked oatmeal.

Worse, their skins were brightly colored in an appetizing fashion, green for the males and orange for the women. How could I resist? They even had respective flavors, the green being for kiwifruit and the orange for banana.

Regardless, their entire race was extinguished. I suppose I should have felt bad, but it was kind of hard to when I was still miffed about their total failure to mention their inherent laxative properties. Seems to me that is something one is duty-bound to issue a disclaimer about.

At the very least.

Jerry Van Dyke's Faith in "My Mother the Car" Was as Misplaced as John Hellins Quick at the 2015 Consumer Electronics Show

The fact that my life was pretty lame became abundantly clear when I found myself spending yet another Tuesday afternoon playing Taboo with the characters from *Gilligan's Island*. You know, that Parker Brothers game where you've got to get people to say the word on the card without interpretively dancing it or the other related ones? It's pretty ubiquitous in competitive full-contact bocce ball circles, so I'm sure you're familiar with it.

Ginger and Mary Ann make a pretty good team. Opposites though they may claim to be as far as taking the country off the aluminum standard, I think they plot and send secret messages encoded in fiber optic cables they made out of wet sand during the Tet Offensive. How else would they get the term "rescue" so fast? It's almost as if they'd been thinking about the word beforehand.

And you knew it was only a matter of time until Gilligan swallowed an entire coconut, along with the two orangutans and Dobie Gillis holding it. That happened the last forty-seven times we played, so it was kind of hard to still believe it was an accident. Where does he even get them? There's not a palm tree, or a bongo-drum-supply emporium, for thousands of miles.

Truthfully, I think it had something to do with all those Spanish *telemarketing* calls he kept getting from that Cuban area code, the ones he got up and opened and shut the window shades a bunch of times after.

The worst was how much the Skipper bitched about getting paired up with the giant spider from "The Pigeon" episode. Sure, it couldn't talk, but everyone had to get paired up on a team with *somebody*. We weren't in Belgium.

What? Did you think I meant only the major characters? Are you some kind of Hayek economics school *Gilligan's Island* elitist? Unfriend me and the entire starting lineup for the 1979 Chicago Bears right now if so, because I have no room in my pickup truck for sandwiches having braunschweiger and no lettuce.

That sort of thing isn't in keeping with the true spirit of *Gilligan's Island* at all or Taboo.

Four Out of Five Peter and the Wolfs Recommend Brushing with Ipana Toothpaste

Say what you want about Muzak, but it never destroyed my teeth and gouged up the walls of my mouth. At least, not as far as I remember. The middle eighties are pretty much of a blur for me, something related to my severe Pop-Tart frosting overdose, so I can't be completely sure. Still, it must not have been then either if I still had teeth to be wrecked now.

My dentist decided Musak was for suckers, you see. Couldn't stand the relaxed blandness anymore. Maybe it was a midlife crisis, or the results of an especially persuasive Rick Steves PBS pledge drive. Regardless, he decided he wanted some *real* music. He didn't go for Slayer like any cultured person would have, decided to slum it and go for a more classical style bent instead.

It moved him, which may not have been what the average patient wants when a dentist has picks and drills and industrial scale shop power tool benches going in one's mouth.

Prokofiev's "Dance of the Knights" proved to be a particular problem. My dentist simply could not sit still, jumping all around and singing words that weren't even there. He waved his arms wildly, which would have been fine had they not been in control of all those implements at the time. Some damage may have been done, though all accidentally. Of course.

Who needs a transfusion during their biannual cleaning? Sutures? Bone grafts? It was a good thing I always used gas during my cleaning or I might really have gotten worried. Not office supplied, I brought my own. Unleaded.

The slower parts helped at least. He realized at that point what he'd just done in his manic musical passion and tried to ameliorate, kept me from dying in that leaned back

Naugahyde chair. Another booming triumphant section just popped up next though and it started all over again.

That appointment was something right out of *Five Little Peppers and How They Grew*. A total bloodbath, I'm telling you. Margaret Sidney must have had a similar problem. Funny, since she was dead not long after Sergei was born. Maybe her dentist heard an early draft.

Luckily, my insurance covered all the repairs…if not anesthetic. Still, I should seek out a less passionate dental surgeon. There are simply some times where I'd prefer to relax. Not everything needed to exalt and excite the soul.

Especially at the expense of dentition.

Jim Fowler Keeps Ringing my Doorbell and Running Before I Can Fix the Martini

I became a prophet last month in the lobby of my office building on my way into work. I was walking through and noticed something green on the gray granite floor. At first, I thought it was a stick-bug, but then I realized it was a praying mantis dressed in gold-lined blue silk robes. That's what I get for taking my "How to Identify a Stick-Bug" course at Kaplan University instead of going to a real school. You get what you pay for, regardless of the excessive rates at which you pay.

Anyway, I went to the security desk to see if they had an original mint-condition copy of *Action Comics* No. 1. I figured the little mantis wouldn't last long on the busy floor of an office building, the average person not being as devoted to mantid conservation as I, and I needed something on which to carry the little guy.

I certainly wasn't going to touch him. I wasn't that committed.

That's when Carol charged me with my sacred mission. Turned out Carol was a she, males already having had their heads bitten off by that point in the season, just like human males around February fifteenth. In fact, she was the goddess queen of the mantids and I was thenceforth to spread the word of her buggy holiness throughout the eastern portions of downtown Denver.

Apparently, her holy power didn't extend to Lakewood.

I was to inform people that they would worship Carol by filling their windshield wiper reservoirs with Janet Lee brand root beer. Such was how Carol defeated the dung beetles from Canaan and the act was sacred to her. If humanity pleased her, she would square dance all summer while they gathered food and worked hard. If they did not, she would bite their heads off and that would make for a cold winter indeed. Mankind was to beware *The Coldest Winter Ever*.

I quipped to Carol that it sounded as if she was confusing the ant and the grasshopper fable with mantid documentaries, as well as Sister Souljah, but Carol told me to hush. I also thought Norman Lear had the rights to that as a sitcom, but I said nothing. Not only was the gun she was pointing at me after my first quip unambiguously requesting my further silence, I wasn't qualified to give legal advice to insects anyway. I decided not to risk the unauthorized practice of Carmen Miranda without an explicit invitation at that point, at least barring lowering of the weapon.

Mind you, Carol didn't have vocal cords. She spoke through a security guard who was hiding behind a rolling nativity set that was hanging out in the lobby as I carried her to a hydroponic teflonated marijuana planter outside. It might seem that he was tricking me and throwing his voice using that cheap ventriloquism kit he got from the Johnson Smith Company catalog, but I knew it was all the work of Carol. I was no fool.

In fact, that's why she chose me as her prophet, that and how I could eat an entire pack of Starburst at one time without having to swallow, or remove the wrappers. People were always impressed by that.

God knows I am.

The Hardest Part of Italian Cooking to Master is the Way Garlic Changes Matter States When You Switch Verb Tenses

The greatest trick Conagra ever pulled was convincing everyone that spaghetti was something made rather than an invertebrate that grew in South America. That way, no one felt as bad as they consumed the rainforests to extract it, along with the wild baloney colonies. After the audacity of that undertaking, the most impressive thing was the sheer scope of their deception. Hundreds of years of history, entire industries of fake pasta-makers and packaging factories, all a sham.

Chef Boyardee knew the truth but wisely kept quiet to avoid assassins.

Spaghetti was first discovered in the seventeen-hundreds by Sean Connery on location filming *Medicine Man*. It grew like grass, but sentiently waved itself to ward off predator approach in the politest fashion possible. For a time, it was thought to have therefore originated in Canada, though spaghetti doesn't have bones with which to leave a fossil record, so no one other than Erich von Däniken could really be sure.

That's the only way modern scholars knew a lot of things, such as the complete list of episodes for *The Facts of Life*.

Of course, spaghetti wouldn't grow in captivity. There's something against that in their contract. Thus, the only way to get it is to send the massive chaff separator combines through the natural spaghetti fields. It destroys the entire settlement and leaves the land unable to bear spaghetti young for three generations, but God help us it tastes so good.

Wars have been fought over the naming rights to the spaghetti noodle. Eighteen of the last thirty-six Crimean

Wars alone, just to give some examples. Imagine then the geopolitical importance to the world of access to spaghetti itself. I'd say it determined much of the course of Western civilization, but I wouldn't want to slight that guy named Earl who delivers Yoo-Hoo to the Amoco station on Federal.

That would never do.

But someday the rainforests will be used up and the spaghetti fields will run dry. At the rate Vince McMahon is going, it could even be within our lifetime.

I only hope you can make do with rigatoni.

The Truth is Out There and it Wants Two Dollars or it Isn't Going Away

It was another *X-Files* episode where the beginning of the show is the end, so I had to drink the entire bottle again. I'd been playing the *X-Files* drinking game. Unfortunately, I didn't drink alcohol anymore since that incident with the secretary of state at the Georgia Tech Guy Fawkes Day and Homecoming Celebration game, so I had to guzzle a mixture of Pepto-Bismol and white shoe polish instead. I had water, but dear God I wasn't going to drink that. I wasn't crazy.

Fox Mulder had once again woken up vandalized in front of the reflecting pool on the National Mall, Washington Monument side. He thought he'd been abducted by aliens and his memory wiped, but after a convoluted investigation at the top levels of government complete with mournful and soulful looks as well as a few pieces of French Silk pie at Village Inn it was revealed that he'd insulted a group of accountants on vacation from Akron while getting hammered on Chambord at Chili's. Once more. They got mad when he kept calling them number plumbers and tying the laces of their bedroom slippers together, so they drew integration symbols all over his face and dumped him in the water once he blacked out.

First to pass out at accountant parties is always in for it.

It wasn't too bad though. There wasn't much Pepto and polish left in my bottle by that point. The previous episode had been the one where Skinner went in for a root canal and said "Attthhh" a hundred and eighty-seven times when the dentist working on him asked what he did for a living. That used up most of my supply, even at one drink a shot, so chugging the rest wasn't too hard.

I'd needed something to do, what with being let go from the Senate due to downsizing. Well, they said that, but I suspected it had something to do with roll call establishing that they had a hundred and four members. Some of those states never could count real well, and President Lenny Bruce was never going to stand for it. They had to take care of it quick on the down low.

But what else was I going to do with my day? That black-market heart transplant operation clinic I was going to run on blow-up dolls out of my house wasn't scheduled to start for a week, and my cable had been shut off due to political differences. I had all those *X-Files* DVDs, so I had little other choice but to play the game even if I didn't drink.

To be honest, I'd kind of forgotten that you could watch the *X-Files* without drinking. Now I need more shoe polish or my shoes are going to look scuffed.

The French Have Been Serving Us Pencil Shavings for Years and Insisting It's Coffee

François Hollande tried to make Manwich in my kitchen this morning. President of France or not, he still has to take his turn cooking if he wants to be roommates. Still, what are they teaching in those French schools? Do they even cover any physics?

He should have known better.

After all, the first law of sloppy joes states that in a closed universe Manwich can neither be created nor destroyed, only change forms. What made Hollande think he could play god? We won't even get into the problems caused by the Manwich Least Squares Hiking Backpack-Unpacking Division theory. Dude was doomed before he started.

I'm helpful though, so I ordered him a quart bag of powdered goldstone. That's over eighty percent fossilized Manwich by volume, and can be used to culture up a whole new colony in less than a week. It isn't FDA approved as a sourdough starter like seventies artificial corkboard platform heels, but it's a heck of a lot more sanitary…and Hollande knows as well as anyone that the government is really just out to get you anyway.

That's the only possible explanation for the popularity of *The Cannonball Run.*

In a pinch, we could have also mined Manwich from the neighbor's yard. They've held so many Bolivian-style rugby practices over there that it's just become embedded in the soil. Our Theremin is on the fritz though, and it costs a fortune to rent since all the mesothelioma decisions, so it was best that I had that goldstone source. Gwen Paltrow hasn't let me down yet.

But all that still left us with what to do for breakfast right then, so we went to Waffle House, of course. Hollande is big on the foie gras they do there, and I do enjoy their hash browns. Also, he digs the fact they don't force him to wear any pants.

He's simply comfier that way.

Ideas: Where to Get Them and What to Do When They Won't Leave

People are always asking me where I get my ideas. I've never really understood that. I mean, I run into them all over the place: supermarkets, taxis, parties, begging for spare change on street corners, orgies, drunk tanks, you know… all sorts of every day places. Frankly, the biggest problem is getting rid of the worthless ones.

For example, take the one I ran into back in March. I was at the biannual convention in Tucson for people who like to use the word "nipple" inappropriately. Advance reports suggested this one wasn't going to amount to much new, but I figured I'd go anyway just to get some of the obligatory networking out of the way. Put in a little face time in the industry and what not, just to keep my name fresh in everyone's mind.

About the time I'd had as much pointless handshaking and business card exchanging as I could stomach, I headed to the refreshment table for a well-deserved break and some free stale pretzels. There was already an idea hanging out when I got there, opening and chugging one can of Diet Coke after another.

"Hey," he gasped between cartridges. "How's it going, guy?"

"Good," I replied perfunctorily while trying to pretend to be deeply engaged in the debate between a bear claw and a cruller. "Not doing too bad at least."

I was not, needless to say, though I will say it anyway, anxious to get into it with this idea. He was dressed up in faded brown corduroy and the Battle of Hastings. The soles of his shoes were peeling off and the Magna Carta hung out of one of his torn pockets. Clearly, he was a bad idea if I'd ever seen one. Maybe even *Harold & Kumar Go to White Castle* bad.

"Working with anybody right now?" He wiped mustard

from his fingers on the checkered paper tablecloth, though none of the snacks on the table included any mustard. "You look like a classy sort. Maybe we should hook up sometime."

"Sure," I replied, stuffing pretzels into my mouth to make it clear I wasn't really seriously considering such. "Maybe someday."

"Really, we should," the idea belched. "I bet you'd be right up my alley. Into weenie dogs?"

"Isn't everyone?"

I pretended to catch sight of someone across the room right then. "Ben! Hey, Ben," I shouted to no one. "Where've you been hiding, you old dog? Sorry, got to run," I hastily told the idea before charging purposefully but aimlessly across the room. Then I ducked into the can and cleared out of that snooze-fest as soon as the coast was clear.

What was I supposed to do? I'd never work with that idea. He'd ruin me. Still, I didn't want to come out and actually say that. No need to be rude, right? We weren't making a deal. I was just being polite.

Or, that's what I thought until the idea pounded on my door.

He charged right on into my condo, carrying a see-through wicker suitcase of old Scholastic magazines and my grandmother's antique silverware when I opened the door. Half asleep from an afternoon nap as I was, he was already kicking back on my beige living room couch and watching reruns of *The Beverly Hillbillies* before I realized what was happening.

"Hey…what are you doing?"

"Settling in!" The idea scratched his crotch (inside whatever underwear the idea might have been wearing) with my remote control. "We got work to do and these things don't happen overnight. Got myself ready to just crash here so we could work round the clock."

I stood there, staring at the revolting little guy. I had to do something; I had to get rid of him quick.

"Well…I'm actually in the middle of a project right now," I stammered, desperately trying to think of a way to get him out my door. "It could be quite a while before I'm ready to get down to something else."

"No problem, boss," he retorted, blowing his nose on my Herman Melville commemorative lace coffee coasters. "I got nothing but time. We'll just be roomies until you get around to it."

Then he switched the channel to a three-day *Toddlers & Tiaras* marathon. Clearly, he was settling in pretty deep. I retreated upstairs just to get away from his smell of old fish and Emily Brontë.

I mean, how else should I have handled the situation? The idea was obviously unstable. His choices in television revealed that if nothing else. There was a chance he'd get violent if I tried to throw him out myself.

The police certainly wouldn't be any help. They tended to stay out of idea-related conflicts. "Purely a domestic matter" they'd say. Too many people invited an idea in and then thought better of it later for law enforcement to get involved. No, ideas were outside police marching orders as far as they were concerned.

So…I was stuck. I couldn't just make him leave and I sure couldn't actually work with him. My only option was to wait him out and hope he got bored.

By the second week, though it was clear that waiting wasn't going to work too well. I'm not sure the idea had even noticed. He just watched TV atrocities, drank all of my Bisquick pancake mix, and made macramé sculptures out of my used mint dental floss. He even alphabetized the words in my first edition copy of the complete works of James Joyce. I guessed that this idea really did have nothing better to do.

My work was starting to seriously suffer. After all, I couldn't bring a decent idea home with that hobo parked on my couch. What would it look like? All the good ideas would be out of there faster than Mark Twain at a James Fenimore Cooper convention. Whatever kinky plan they'd think I was roping them into, they would want no part of it.

Finally, when I'd had all I could stand, I went and got my tools. Now, I don't mean my normal ones. I drug out that real bastard of a set from where it rusted on the shelf in the garage. One way or another, this idea was getting taken out.

He sat up when I stomped in and pulled the plug on *Dancing with the Stars*. I positioned a chair on the other side of the glass coffee table from him and grinned. His head bobbed as he swallowed sharply.

"What you got there, boss? Thinking of doing a little renovating before we get down to business?"

"Nah," I laughed hollowly, slapping my knee with a jerky motion. "I thought it was time that we embark upon our mutual little enterprise here. No time like the present, right?"

I took out my foot-long cattle gutter out of the dented iron box and dropped it on the table. The nicks in the hard metal blade glistened as it fell.

"Only, I'm considering a different direction than daschunds. Something along the epic line. Maybe three thousand pages of consciousness stream unformed dream logic babble with a hint of poetic inversion. Real high-level groundbreaking academic fiction kind of stuff. We'll need serious gear to take that on. Maybe lawyers."

The idea stared as I tossed the bone saw next to the gutter. The rib retraction ripper came next, followed by the skin hooks. He even gasped a little when I brought out the reciprocating centrifuge cartilage/fluid separator.

"Yeah," I went on, pretending to check the high-pressure formaldehyde pump for coagulants, "no fun and games on this one. Pain and sweat kind of writing for years on end by candlelight, right? That's the only thing for guys of our caliber. None of that readable excrement. No fluff."

It was the testicle corer that really got him though, what with all the gears and serrations. I held that up in front of the idea and he was already halfway out the condo.

"To tell the truth, boss," he called over his shoulder as he ran, "I've got a few short pieces I need to ride sidecar on before I can commit to something long-term like this. I'm your man once I get all that wrapped up. I'll call you!"

Before I knew it, I was free. The medieval assortment went back to its place in the garage and I finally got back to work. All in all, it was just another day.

Extreme though it may seem, this is what you have to sometimes resort to in order to get an unwanted idea out of your house. Just start putting it through the paces like it could really amount to something. The bad ones will check out by noon instead of enduring that kind of thing. Trust me, I know.

There's Still Only so Much Vomit Dark Multi-Colored Shag Carpet Can Hide

My parents told me there were crows in our attic, so I used my plastic Fisher Price tool set to convert my double sliding door closet into a pneumatic elevator so I could go up and have a look. It cut down on the storage space in my room a bit, but I didn't care about that so much given that I was three. I simply kept all my stuff on the floor anyway, so it wasn't much of a problem. The crows only turned out to be some band that wanted to bring back bell-bottoms though, so I boarded up the shaft with recycled Amazon boxes and went onto other projects.

For instance, I put together a car for my Baby Secret doll out of an old Similac box, Mutual of Omaha tax documents, clear Parkay lids, and mostly unused brass paper fasteners. She didn't really have anywhere to drive, but this was the late seventies so everyone needed a car. Of course, the car got less than optimal miles to the gallon, and the fuel crisis was on, so I had a neighbor carve a canoe out of mustard and old oak twigs. After his garage burned down for the third time, I decided to scrap that whole deal as well and let the ungrateful brat walk.

Jimmy Carter simply made any wide-scale transportation plan infeasible.

The currency production set up was a better bet, crayon drawings done by rejects from the *Captain Kangaroo* show using flesh-colored earwax on scraps of my fuzzy textured gold and green wallpaper. To avoid trouble with the feds we weren't counterfeiting, simply subcontracting the job of the mint. However, the value of the dollar ended up falling so low eventually that I had to abandon that as well, even though I still hadn't paid anyone. Plus, we needed the dining room to eat Thanksgiving Toblerone dinner.

I tried a waterpark using plastic measuring cups shaped

like members of The Partridge Family in my room, resulting in a bit of a severe death mold problem. I knew I shouldn't have used city water. Still, it wasn't as if I had the hazmat gear to work with anything from the Missouri, and anhydrous hydrazine makes my throat itch. There were only so many choices I had.

The swami gig fell apart since I was a Rocky Mountain Synod Three-Quarters Jumping Jam Lutheran. Genetically engineering pleather owls kept making me throw up in bed. A brief career as Spiderman ended with a Roundup motor oil spill in the backyard.

Nothing quite worked out completely.

Luckily, I finally started kindergarten. That came with problems of its own, but at least those failures stemmed from the flawed plans of other people. We could all pretend that I could be doing great things if only I had the time.

Sometimes that's enough.

Tootie Seemed Sweet, But Her Lust for the Blood of Nebraskans and Her Annexation of the Hobbit Homelands Eventually Destroyed *The Facts of Life*

Gold became a much more significant part of my life after Dom DeLuise started trying to use his transcendental meditationalist mind control powers to force me to canvas the third municipal pudding and toothpaste district for McGovern. I shouldn't have pissed him off by breaking into the inverted pyramid tomb to use the mummified corpse of Pharaoh Burt Reynolds the fourth in the River City Roundup parade, but that still doesn't give Dom an excuse. Only by gold plating my hair with specially rigged cans of Aqua Net could I be safe.

Let me tell you, it was no easy matter.

I mean, only the old PCB cans were any good. Do you know how hard it is to find that stuff since Don Henley took over the EPA in that bloody Boy Scout coup? I had to get a special dispensation from the pope, and that alone was harder than the time I convinced Peter Fonda to do a sequel to *Easy Rider*. Oh yeah, gold is also expensive.

Most of what I needed was obtained when I hit the Colorado State Capitol building dome with a novelty-sized potato peeler. It all flaked right into the Santa Ana winds, which was mysterious to begin with since they aren't in Colorado, but that's why I'd posted Elliott Gould on top of Republic Plaza. Gould attracts gold, as any serious hard rock scientist will tell you. Elliott had to die from heavy metal poisoning for the scheme to work, but I knew sacrifices had to be made. Elliott was aware too, though he might have made a different choice had I actually given him an option.

Screw that hippy though. He wasn't the one who had to deal with Dom's psionic abilities.

Granted, gold is a lot easier to come by since they discovered it playing hide and seek in the used fryer oil at McDonald's. Still, it's really gross to get in there and get it. I'd rather give up Elliott than have to spend that much of my day washing my hands.

Besides, what would we then use to make potato-flavored Slim Jims?

No, Elliott had to die. He could always just have taken out Dom for me with that casino-cracking crew of loveable singing grade-school orphans he has. If he wanted to keep up that *it's only a movie* garbage, then I just didn't feel sorry for him.

You and Dom shouldn't either.

Exxon Stole my Oatmeal

A crack formed in the pavement at my bus stop last week. The earth was wounded and its blood—crude oil—burbled out. I called the Republican National Committee, figuring it was their sort of thing, but they said they were getting out of that since there was so much bad press. They were going into solar and wind just as soon as they could figure out how to lock down rights on the weather and the sun.

Pretty sure it was Jesse Helms that I talked to.

Had a hard time getting to work in the mornings though. I had to straddle the crack with my feet on both sides opposite where the oil would flow. The city built a drain, but no one ever came out to actually patch. Seemed like the crack widened each day unless my legs were shrinking again.

Neighborhood kids kept running up and throwing their lit torches under me too. Don't know why their parents kept buying them those things, but it flamed that crude right up. If I hadn't been wearing my *Sanford and Son* commemorative asbestos long underwear I'd have been baked for sure.

Damn torch kids.

But then I got thinking that I needed to heal the earth, was visited at night by the photocopied essence of Joan Baez and the Dani people of Papua, New Guinea as they appeared that time together on *The New Scooby-Doo Mysteries*. Needles for the stitches kept bending in the cement though, and them stupid butterfly strips never would quite reach across.

It was a hell of a thing, and I was going through a lot of shoes.

And then it simply sealed over all on its own. Made me feel like a real doof. I never knew asphalt was only crude oil that sat in the sun long enough while being cussed at by some guy with dirty shoes. No one in road construction ever admits that.

Still, I'm going to start taking the train instead. Other than Jesse James and the Apple Dumpling Gang, what's the worst that could happen there?

Lord Rutherford's Gold Foil Disco Suits Were a Big Hit in Vegas But the Beryllium Earrings Were Simply Gaudy

It's unfortunate that my friend Fred has a mirror running the length of his bathroom wall. People keep getting trapped in it and we have a heck of a time getting them out. We're running out of shaving cream. It's enough to make us take out the mirror, but then people couldn't fix their hair. That would never do.

There's something about the full room replicated like that. A moment's distraction is all that's necessary for the mind to forget which side of the glass it's on, and then the soul's attraction to quicksilver takes over. The body can't exist without a soul, so it follows along as well. You know, all that seventh-grade human growth and development type stuff.

It's really pretty basic.

Other rooms don't seem to have the same issue, but Marie Curie's pioneering bathroom science research showed lavatories to be particularly vulnerable to side switching kinds of distractions. Something about the optics and porcelain to drywall ratio, toxic toothpaste fumes, and ceramic tile codependent atomic bonds. That, and the mental distancing we all do to avoid being overly disgusted by our own intimate bodily processes. For vanity reasons if nothing else, one look and dinner parties are halted yet again.

It plays hell on the timing of the courses.

Though, it's not as if there isn't room in the mirror. People are comfortable and all. Sure, it's two-dimensional, but the light wave reflections inside the glass makes that mimic the conditions of three. It's all light anyway, so those trapped still think that they can move around. They just can't get out, since the door in the mirror image is not a physically operational object.

It sucks, but there you go.

We have to storm in with the Shop-Vac when it happens, reconstitute their particles in the blender with a little bit of chunky-style peanut butter. Like on *Star Trek*. It's not a big deal, but it does tend to leave guests swearing lifelong blood vendettas against their host and everyone who ever voted for Hubert Humphrey.

Fred was about ready to take the mirror out anyway, say to hell with winning the Charles Atlas Most Dynamic Home and Garden competition, which we'd lost for sixteen years running anyway due to Electoral College corruption, but I had a better idea. We're going to open up the wall behind that mirror so people can just walk on out from either side.

I foresee no problems with that.

People Got Their Shopping Done Much Faster After President Kanye Kardashian Replaced All Muzak with the Main Theme From *Deathstalker II*

Life was sure better once Kevin Bacon started driving around in that E-Z-GO golf cart selling liquor in Dixie cups everywhere. I'm not sure how he got a license to do that, particularly given the open container/wax paper cup thing, or how he seemed to be everywhere in the world at once like Santa Claus, but the KGB told me to stop asking so many questions unless *Jeopardy!* called me back. "Just go with it, dude," they said, popping me a cold one they'd bought from Kevin special for me on his last pass of Kiev (beer was cans of Red Dog, the sole exception to the Dixie cup standard).

It was only a single one, and not even Old Style, so don't start thinking they bought me off or anything.

But life, man. Life. Kevin and his cart certainly changed it. Thursday was a perfect example. The FDIC had cornered me in a Hostess CupCake delivery alley behind the Washington Monument because I wouldn't stop comparing Richard Nixon to natural birthing techniques and they were going to repossess my kneecaps. Kevin came rolling right up though and frightened them away with a reticulated particle accelerator disguised as a recreational potato clock. I didn't know where he'd gotten it, but he sure saved my butt that time.

That wouldn't be the only illustration either. I couldn't forget the way he drove in and built housing for rich congressmen using only old boxes of Kraft macaroni & cheese. He changed the course of city council politics forever that day, let me tell you. Granted, the later fire left us without any political leadership at a very difficult time, what with the cartoon tigers and all, but I didn't think you could blame Kevin for that part. Dude could only be expected to do so much.

Though, I did concede that not all the life alterations were for the good. He did key every automobile in a tri-state area as he wandered around on his little cart. Then he stabbed Spencer Pratt with a grapefruit pick after the police deputized him to ask what was up. Transformation always involved upheaval, however, and we wouldn't have wanted to be like Duncan Hines and simply avoid all change categorically.

What would the 2016 Oscars ceremony have been like if we had?

The constant liquor supply part didn't affect much, of course. How could it? Clark Gable had been doing that shtick on a bicycle for years already. It wasn't exactly the most original business plan.

Not anymore.

Somebody Misplaced Montana

Somebody misplaced Montana. They made everyone look under their desks to see if it had fallen, but only old bubble gum, notes about Bobby riding his BMX bike without a shirt, and the Hapsburg dynasty were down there. Montana wasn't.

Nobody knew how long it'd been gone. We'd had our heads down during recess because of the War of 1812, so we hadn't noticed. Only when someone realized the North Dakota/Idaho Hostess CupCake run was shorter was the absence noted. We all agreed it could have been that way for a while.

Businesses located in Billings changed their address to Coeur d'Alene, a formality really. People based in Missoula weren't affected because there weren't any. It was all reasonable and prudent.

I bet Corey had stuffed Montana in his overall pocket when no one was looking. He was an angry kid, always stealing stuff and jamming it in that damn pocket. States, nuclear reactors, even a child's sense of wonder. He didn't want any of that crap, but there it all was. In his pocket. I didn't say anything, though. Montana was no reason to be a snitch.

At first, the principal was mad; he'd booked a vacation in Butte that summer. A Beanie Babies safari set to coincide with the annual balsa wood airplane and *Brokeback Mountain* cosplay convention. They told us he wouldn't let us leave until Montana was returned, but then he just said he was disappointed in us sent us home without our pineal glands.

He couldn't prove anything without resorting to a search or a supermarket magazine psychic anyway. Besides, it was only Montana.

Obscure Ex-Presidents and Their Merry Toy-Making Elves

Former President Benjamin Harrison, for Christmas this year I'd like an Incredible Hulk life-sized Playdoh bone spur removal surgery play set. Not the off-brand generic version, the real deal only. That knock off causes cancer in lab rats that are addicted to recreational use of dental X-rays, and I've been a good boy.

You might wonder why I'm telling you what I want instead of Santa Claus. The guys at the office recently told me that Santa doesn't exist, so I can't call him. I know you're real, even if you died in 1893, and you look the most like Santa of all the ex-presidents so you're the one I'm asking.

Of course, you might not be wondering…being dead and all.

I'd also like a national forest. I heard you were involved in getting those going, so I figured you could hook me up. I'd like either the National Leftover Liposuction Waste Prairie Reserve or the United States Shut Up Donny Ski Slope and Breaker Wave Reservoir, but I'd be willing to settle for Yellowstone. Just not the Grand Canyon, please. We both know that hasn't been the same since the Fiber Communists started stashing their worn-out Bart Simpson dolls there.

I mean, really.

If you promise to bring me what I ask, I'll in turn promise to set out a nice plate of McKinley tariffs and a tasty cold glass of Ovaltine for you. I know how tiring Christmas can be and how a little refreshment can be in order, particularly when you've had to fight David Hasselhoff for the heavyweight boxing championship of the world yet again. I swear, that guy will never learn…no matter how many concussions you give him.

I bet all that singing in German is what made him so nuts.

Anyway, come through for me, former President Benjamin

Harrison. All the guys at the office say your administration was below-average, but I know they're just jealous you got to represent the Republic of Venezuela against the United Kingdom in that royalty dispute over X-Men collectible anti-depressant infused BVDs. I know you're the man. Don't let me down, even if you are dead.

Otherwise next year I'll call on Millard Fillmore.

How Can Brexit be my Fault if my Refrigerator Manual Told Me to Invade Belize?

For optimal use of the Official Steven Seagal Weed Wacker and Portable Underwear Embroidery product, clip the string spool to the hub at the center of "Steven Seagal's" head prior to connecting your wacker to an AC outlet. Do not instead unwind the moist plastic string from the spool and attempt to trade chunks of it to Washington D.C. political natives for gold or local furs. Non-approved string usage voids your wacker's warrantee.

Wackers should be used to trim grasses, small shrubs, and other non-woody plants having stalk diameters of no more than fifteen millimeters. Wackers should not be used as aquatic vehicular transport for seventeenth-century parties of conquistadors traveling the Amazon River on Sundays in search of the fabled cities of disco gold. Any use of your wacker as aquatic transport for traveling the Amazon river in search of the fabled cities of disco gold voids your wacker's warrantee and may subject you to criminal prosecution regardless of your historical time period, the day of the week, or your conquistador status. The manufacturer expressly takes no official position on whether or not you are a conquistador, but come on.

The manufacturer also makes no representations, express or implied, as to whether or not you may be attacked by juvenile delinquent harbor seals while using your wacker, whether in approved or unapproved manners. Conditions and results inherently vary, and the manufacturer takes no responsibility, beyond any imposed by applicable law, for the acts of seal miscreants. If the user is attacked by seals, of any species and/or of any age, the manufacturer recommends seeking the assistance of Queen Elizabeth the first or the nearest civil aquatic mammal authority.

Do not eat your Official Steven Seagal Weed Wacker and Portable Underwear Embroidery product. Your Official Steven Seagal Weed Wacker and Portable Underwear Embroidery product does not constitute a low-calorie food substitute.

Thank you. Following the above instructions will keep your wacker operating in prime condition for many years of fine service. Or, at least it would if you hadn't bought that Ronco combination ATB/Lunesta-Themed Home Pharmacy last week. Because of that, you'll probably be dead and lying in a ditch within a week.

Honestly, what made you think that was a good idea?

Jacques Cousteau Was On Sealab 2020, But They Had Him in a Monkey Mask Because He Was in Witness Protection at the Time

There wasn't much for me at the antique mall at Saint-Ouen, mostly vintage crotchless codpieces and chèvre Ani DiFranco records, but that changed when I saw an old Futuro house set up as the centerpiece to the place, a sixties concept housing experiment in tiny living originally designed as a ski lodge but looking more like a UFO, so I jumped up on its stairs and screamed throughout the mall:

I am a visitor from another world, much like your own but with more jellybeans, and I want to bring you the intergalactic message of non-stick shag carpeting and hot buttered popcorn oil massage,

because, after all, the Futuro fit the seventies more from a décor standpoint, filled with Andy Warhol looking furniture and toasted cheese squares, gluten-free of course since it was intended to be space age, though only a hundred or so of the homes were ever built and most were vandalized with washable crayons and no bank would issue a car loan for one and many places wouldn't let you mount one anyway because even in the seventies people thought they were kind of ugly and ugly hadn't caught on as a specific style until 1982, Jerry Falwell being a point in fact when he sang:

In heaven, there is no beer, no beer, which is why we drink it here,

but that's when the steps of the Futuro pulled up, taking me and seven agnostic goats with it, and all the lights atop began to strobe around in various post-modern looking ways despite the fact that there had been no lights in place beforehand, and the prefab house lifted off the ground and with a few slight wobbles coasted out of the doors of the run-down mall and soared into the low-hanging sky, because it turned out that Futuros weren't simply forward-looking Swedish pop-art installation pieces from the post World War two era but actually alien craft from a small planetoid out in the Kuiper Belt, the part just left of the buckle, and a voice read out in my mind:

Four score and seven breakfasts ago, I had a sandwich with peanut butter and pickles, no margarine thank goodness, on wheat toast stuffed inside a pepperoni pizza because a snack is a great thing to have while watching television,

because the aliens were long dead due to cirrhosis of the testicles after drinking Wild Irish Rose but their telepathic grail transmitter still worked, the mike line accidentally having been tied into the a.m. sandwich advertising radio station staffed entirely by middle-aged men resembling Dudley Moore who kept breaking in only to say:

Mind you, I was wearing an onion on my belt, which was the style at the time,

which is actually how I got out of the whole mess because it turned out the government had a Farm Aid program specifically for that.

Missy Wore a White Skirt with Pantyhose and I Can't Handle Shoes Right Now

That shoe march was cool, people making their voices heard about global warming while acknowledging the need to keep safe in view of the Paris attacks, but it was too bad that it led to the elephants taking over the world. That put a black mark on all the good feels involved. It's hard not to view the whole thing negatively as a result, at least as long as the elephants didn't remove our temporal lobes to destroy our capacity for independent thought.

We really should have foreseen that it would happen. Ten thousand pairs of shoes sitting alone in a square? Of course, elephants were going to come in and steal them. What else? Then those ten thousand people were helpless.

After all, they had no shoes.

Worse, then the elephants blackmailed them. The elephants threatened to post pictures of the shoes naked online for everyone to see. They really had those poor shoeless people by the balls. How could they not do anything those elephants said?

Just think of the humiliation.

Sure, the world turned out in support of the shoeless. Protest marches were scheduled. The elephants were up all night stealing shoes at that point though. Quickly, the whole world was under their thumb, metaphorically speaking of course. Elephants are digitigrades. It was a worse defeat for mankind than the last time Kevin Costner tried to direct a science fiction movie.

We won't even talk about Ron Howard.

Keep in mind, we're talking about African elephants, not Asian. However, I doubt anyone would be confused. Asian elephant overlords would be ridiculous. Those things had no ambition at all, too laid-back smoking dope on their mom's couches, content to spend their time answering call center phones and watching reruns of *America's Next Top Model.*

People were always predicting the end of humanity, but no one ever thought we'd go out shoeless at the hands of the elephants. I don't see why not though, it made at least as much sense as sentient robots. Elephants don't even need oiling, though they do like it.

Frankly, our only hope is for a competing offensive from the badgers. Badgers would fuck those elephants up.

Maybe they'd even give us back our shoes.

A Totally True Story That Engelbert Humperdinck Will Never Believe Again

Nobody believes that I once beat Larry Bird at basketball, but it's totally true. I popped out from behind the bleachers while he was making a three-point shot and smacked the living crap out of him with a tube sock full of peeled nickels. Larry was a good sport about it and all, but he still got beat.

I firmly maintain that it was "at basketball" since that's what he was playing at the time. Practice still counts.

Of course, no one believes me. I guess I can't blame them since Larry did get Thurgood Marshall to issue that restraining order preventing any person from coming within one hundred feet of believing otherwise. Thurgood wasn't going to do it, the Supreme Court having a long history of disfavoring prior restraint when both consenting parties haven't agreed on a mutual safe word, but he owed Moses Malone a favor.

I have no idea why Moses got involved. Perhaps he wanted to reward Larry for helping him gather all that manna in the mornings. Aaron Malone was certainly no help.

Yeah, Larry was a good sport…but not good enough to avoid seeking legal redress. Maybe I shouldn't have used sour nickels. I really didn't have much of a choice though, Best Buy had a buy-one-get-a-second mail-in rebate at half fifty percent off the price of an unrelated 56K modem sale. The other ones they stocked wouldn't have been compatible with my Herman Miller Aeron office chair, or my Commodore VIC 20.

It was a good beating too, right up there with the greats showcased at the hall of fame in Phoenix. I kept running in, whapping him a bunch of times, and then running off before anyone could grab me. I was too fast for the coaching staff, and by too fast I mean I was naked and covered in Bisquick pancake batter. I call that too fast, wouldn't you?

I bet Larry wouldn't have sweated it at all if the Spanish Infanta hadn't been watching. He was hoping to forge a marriage alliance with her to bolster his military strength against Argyle-Hungary and couldn't appear weak. The worry was for nothing in the end, since the Infanta thought he looked hot soaked in nickels juice.

Rule thirty-four, don't you know.

Still, it's completely true and not a soul buys it. Maybe I'd have had better luck if I hadn't said the exact same thing happened with Hank Aaron just the week before. It's not as if anyone was going to believe that lie anyway.

Hank Aaron doesn't even like basketball.

Marc Summers Instigated the War Between the Bloods and the Crips so He Deserves Everything He Gets

I've got Marc Summers imprisoned in the toilet of my upstairs bathroom. You remember, the host from *Double Dare*? Got a metal colander locked down over the bowl with a Krypton bicycle lock run through apertures I drilled into the porcelain. It isn't exactly a posh accommodation, but it's not as if he's on a level with the Kardashians or anything.

He's only Marc.

Sometimes I go and dump quicklime powder in there after flushing a bunch of times, burn terrible holes in his flesh while I pelt him with lima beans and puréed Hostess Twinkies. You might not think those would get through the holes in the colander real well, but I manage all right given the intensity of my motivation. His screams make me pretty resourceful. "Physical challenge, motherfucker!" I often yell.

The phrase isn't exactly apropos, given that he isn't supposed to be doing anything at the time other than suffering. Not even escaping, particularly after I sawed off his legs with a cheese grater during the competitive tackle bridge tournament I held for Sally Struthers and Ted Nugent, at Ted and Sally's instigation, of course.

No idea what's wrong with those two.

I mean, for me it goes back to the show. I watched and watched, planning for the day I'd get on myself. I figured out all the traps, how to best get the flag on each section. There were always tricks if you could only see them, not get scrambled by the pressure of the show and the fact you were standing in a gigantic lemon meringue pie. Hell, I *trained* for that show. What did they think would happen when it went off the air?

Sure, it came back in other incarnations…but it wasn't the same. Also, I was too old and too porous.

He might not have been thinking of that twenty years later when he tried to pick me up with that lame "Got any Irish in you" line while the Jets game was playing at that corner sweet tea bar, but maybe he should have. Matthew Broderick knew enough to be wary, even if Marc didn't. Thus, into the toilet Marc went.

It's cool though. I've got four bathrooms in my house and only two non-captive people. Sometimes I go a little in each just to make sure things stay even, and you can still use Marc's bathroom if you only need to wash your hands. He's cool with it as long as you don't gawk at the way the quicklime scarred up his face.

Like any of the Hollywood people, Marc can be a little vain.

Seltzer Water was Invented so Geena Davis Could Pretend Like She was Buying Her Children a Healthy Treat When She Really Hated Them and the Way They Spoiled the Spanish-American War for the Netherlands

Ballpark summer 1986: Omaha Royals versus the Oklahoma Zephyrs in Omaha, likely due to special backroom-agreement with the city government of Annapolis. My first baseball game, tickets provided by my elementary school in order to pack in crowds for Waldo to hide in from the Mossad. Never got tickets before because I'd previously gone to a private school run for the kids of families who frequented the Sinclair gas station on Dodge. At least, we thought it was a school. The federal investigation later indicated it might have been a separatist lumberyard. The Royals beat the Zephyrs 8–3 by using Voodoo magic learned from a Beverly Cleary book.

Ballpark summer 1987: Omaha Royals versus the Oklahoma Zephyrs in Omaha (again), rematch because the previous year's game had started before the Zephyr's laundry was fully done. Instead of baseball, confusion led to the match being decided by a drinking contest between Annie Oakley and the Kurgan from the *Highlander* movie. No one remembered to keep score, so Clive Anderson awarded a hundred points to the Royals and none to the Zephyrs because he said no one gave a crap about farm league team games. Gas riots ensued for reasons no one could fathom, but damage was so minimal as to be unnoticed by everyone other than Fritz Leiber.

Ballpark summer 1988: Omaha Royals versus the Oklahoma Zephyrs in Omaha yet again, originally scheduled to be played in Oklahoma but changed at the last minute when the Zephyr's mother wouldn't let them have friends over since they hadn't cleaned their room. I spent most of the game trying to trade state secrets to hot dog vendors for free glasses of semi-sweetened iced tea. That went poorly since other vendors were in charge of drinks. The Royals beat the Zephyrs nine divided by the square root of an undefined quantity roughly equivalent to the number of people who would write in Hubert Humphrey as a joke in the next presidential election instead of Mickey Mouse, but only because the entire Zephyr team went into the stands to beat Gene Siskel for talking to Marion Morrison during play, leaving the Royals unobstructed ability to score. Jail sentences were harsh but fair. That led to a breakdown in the fabric of the space-game schedule.

Ballpark summer 1992: Omaha Royals versus the Oklahoma Zephyrs in Omaha, the Zephyrs having long since stopped being an independent team due to treason charges and only existing as a chump foil for the Royals. I hadn't gone to the ballpark in years, no longer getting free elementary school tickets once I left due to turning pro. Finally talked my way into the stadium without a ticket by handing out free bologna. Things had changed in the years I'd been away. Instead of a diamond, it was a stage inside the Civic Auditorium. Instead of infielders, it was Tool playing *Prison Sex*. I decided I was done with baseball. The Royals won 5–1.

Ballpark summer 3015: Omaha Royals versus the Oklahoma Zephyrs in Omaha, emeritus. I was still in the stadium, having been there since 1994 after I broke down and snuck in to wait for Santa. The rest of the crowd and I regularly prayed for the end times, but the Royals just kept playing the Zephyrs, by that point both teams being entirely staffed by sentient gophers. None of us knew why we could not die. Reagan blamed the Communists, but his rationale was shaky. All we could do was continue to wait for it to stop. Royals won 3–2.

The Movie Frozen is Actually All About Walt's Cryogenic Rejuvenation Chamber and How He Will Return Once Israel is Truly Free From the Necromantic Influence of Jeff Dunham

I knew it sounded opposite of what you'd think, but perhaps I shouldn't have contradicted that Franco-Prussian massage woman when she asked if I wanted a happy ending. The place wasn't supposed to be *that* kind of massage parlor, and I was married to the sandwich mafia anyway, but I also didn't want to be shot by federal marshals after my friends and family had been deported to a Siberian polo resort just before the credits rolled. No Easter egg at the end of those for this movie, though there was a surprise appearance by Batman.

The fact that the massage woman turned out to be Michael Eisner wearing a wig was a big clue. What it was a big clue of I'm not sure, but certainly, it was a big clue of something… perhaps the involvement of pro-computer industry Haitian Libertarians. The wig slipped as he worked my shoulders, revealing a pronounced brow ridge, and there he was.

Michael Eisner.

He told me to call him "Mickey." Said he got his start doing that commercial for Life cereal, though they pronounced his name wrong. Based on that, Genghis Khan hired him as a price-shopper general to subjugate the Amana Colonies. Chaining one atrocity-filled sweeps week victory to another, he managed to assemble a Banana Republic army (the slightly expensive and highly homogenized clothing store, not any South American country) and staged a bloody coup for bocce ball supremacy of Disney.

The choreography and costumes were excellent, but the line delivery was hesitant…and Walt had to die.

At the same time, Disney's quality had gone downhill. People were tuning out. More and more computer-generated schlock, Eisner had no one to tell stories to. That's when he turned to massage, much like Benito Juárez.

So he went undercover and used his demonic blood-magic powers to forcibly tell the stories of those under his evil fingers. Each had a choice of good or bad, that's how the deal with the devil went, and I'd given up the chance for good when I rebuffed his sexual advances. That's what sealed my family's, and Florida's (the character on *Good Times*, not the state), fate.

Of course, don't get me wrong…it was still better than letting that old freak give me a handjob. I mean, come on.

Converse Are Our First Line of Defense Against Undead Aliens

We've got an infestation of the pot dealer's kid from next door in our basement. I think he got in when we answered the door for all those Merle Haggard cassettes we ordered COD from K-Tel. Maybe he wanted to get away from all the particle physics discussions at home, being simply part and parcel of how modern drug deals get done, but he's down there regardless.

It took a little while to notice if I'm being honest. He'd crawled behind an electric organ we'd pushed against the wall and piled microwave ovens atop, one of those old models that lights up the keys to show you how to play Muzak versions of Erich Zann tunes. Laid in a supply of Little Debbie Cosmic Brownies and hundreds of samovars of Oolong tea. It was only when he chanted "Frogs…frogs…grab their necks and wring 'em out! Frogs…frogs…and there's no silence in the night" after we'd gone to bed that we had any clue. By then it was too late, short of calling a triple Ph.D. exterminator who specialized in neoclassical symphonic home instruments.

We were stuck.

After all, it wasn't as if we could dig the little bugger out ourselves. He bit, and pot dealer's kids were a protected species since the Cheech and Chong Comedy Riots of '72. Damn that Strom Thurmond. That meant we couldn't use gas or those metal salad tongs.

There was always a chance at three a.m. when he crawled out to call his broker to keep up on his day trading, but we never managed to get the net in time. We could only see him by the glow in the dark Edsger Dijkstra heads he'd drawn on his boxer shorts, and we always forgot until the last minute that it wasn't just our Honeywell Robotics semi-sentient HVAC system switching on again. It was all just bells and whistles we didn't need anyway, but Emperor Norton ate our user's manual and we couldn't figure out how to turn that off.

He'll probably move on soon though. There's a Manheim Steamroller concert in a couple months and I bet he won't want to miss that. That's what kids are into now, right? Maybe we should toss some free tickets down there to be sure, and some Ziploc bags full of ham salad for him to eat during the show.

We aren't monsters.

Privatization of Public Nuisances is Far and Away Focused on the Color of Money

Tom Cruise moved into the house two doors down from me so I went over with a fruit basket that had cameras hidden inside the oranges to welcome him to the neighborhood. I wasn't with the neighborhood association anymore since they'd managed to link me to the Russians, so this was all on my own. I could do that though. Indicted by the Knights of Malta or not, I had my rights.

Tom stood in the doorway, blocking my view of his foyer. He said: "I suppose you're here to find out if I'm gay."

"Actually, that's your own business and I don't really give a damn, Tom," I replied, "but I'd like to find out more about those secret coal mines in the *Mission: Impossible* movies. We all know you guys had strip pits just off camera in every scene so the audience wouldn't notice them, pulling all that anthracite from the national celluloid reserves. I want to know about that, and how it relates to the rumors of your new transcontinental model railroad empire."

But he already had an injunction waiting to go for me, a gag order issued by Judge Reinhold, so he didn't have to admit crap. I couldn't ask any further either, not unless I wanted to spend more time in that chilly gulag in Tribeca. However, I wasn't going to give up that easily.

"I bet you want to know what the real tenets of Scientology are," he sighed, bobbing and weaving around in the doorway to keep whatever was clunking out of sight.

"Couldn't care less, Tom," I confided, "but why don't you spill the beans on that pyramid of severed alpaca heads you built on Oprah's couch between takes for your Honey Bunches of Oats commercial? We'd all like to get a little more info on the whereabouts of those people from the Roanoke colony, and how they turned into camelids.

But trade secrets were trade secrets. Even I had to respect that, regardless of how much my curiosity may have gotten the better of me. Loose lips lived in stone glass houses and all that, a bird in the hand called for an erection lasting for more than four hours. I wasn't a complex jackass or anything.

"You're probably wondering why *Eyes Wide Shut* was so awful," Tom whispered, putting his hand over my eyes, one finger over my lips, so I couldn't see what was crawling through the hall behind him, "why it pretended to be so sinister when it was only a bunch of rich people fucking."

"Not really, Tom," I cut him off. "I only want to say 'hi' and tell you to stay off my lawn." Then I pushed him back inside and slammed the front door. That was probably enough to keep him contained. I nailed it shut a wee bit to make absolutely sure.

I mean, there were property values to think of.

In the Beginning, Good Always Overpowered Taxidermied Chipmunks and Free Frosting Wednesdays at Applebee's

Summer? I remember Summer. She was that hot chic in my zero-gravity creative writing class in high school. Not sure why they taught like that, since it didn't improve the writing at all, but it sure made it difficult to get lines down on paper. All the coffee and goatees kept floating away. Mostly, I spent the periods ogling Summer…who didn't have a goatee anyway. I think she had coffee, but that might have been a mixture of Crystal Clear Pepsi and old Bostitch mechanical pencil shavings instead.

It was kind of hard to tell from where I was bolted in.

I remember running into her at a National Pickle Week drinking party that some amateur bowling alley mechanic enthusiasts on the school bus invited me to. They were only trying to get me to vote for the Mann Act, but it was nice to be invited for once…even if the cessation of death three months prior had caused fermentation to stop and thus no one could drink because there wasn't any liquor to be had. We still had fun watching that *Robin Hood* animal cartoon and wrecking whoever's house they had borrowed for the party, though that did lead to Hulk Hogan biting Summer's ass.

I mean, even if she did bend over in those *Dukes of Hazzard* commemorative denim shorts and put it right in his face, that was still no excuse. He wasn't supposed to be playing a heel and should have asked permission first regardless.

No, wait…that was Mimi's ass that Hogan bit, not Summer's. Don't know why I'm talking about that if it didn't have anything to do with Summer. Mimi was a knockout too, but she certainly wasn't Summer…as all girls who weren't

Summer weren't.

Everybody knows Summer.

Though I don't mean biblically since she wasn't comfortable with that outside of Tennessee. Sure, there was that time the police found her with Abraham and his child on the hill by that altar, claiming God said to kill the kid, but you can't call the situation biblical simply due to a few similarities. There's lots of things in the Bible and we'd never get anywhere if we started labeling everything that bore any faint resemblance at all.

It just isn't the same.

But Summer though, Summer was a cool chic. If it hadn't been for that year after high school when she took the interim president emeritus of Conagra hostage in the Leavenworth Street 7–Eleven to protest pudding prices, I'd wonder what she was up to these days. I may not be the smartest man, but I know when the NSA makes it safer not to ask.

Even for Summer.

The Exchange Rate Between He-Man Figurines and G.I. Joe Was Heavily Dependent on Current Relations Between the Soviet Union and Brazil in the Arena of Futuristic Laser Skateboard Combat

"Ladies and gentlemen, I'm not sure if you have ever stopped to consider the many advantages of being able to make your own Smurfs. Imagine, at the very least, no longer being dependent on the Middle East for your home Smurf supply. That alone would change the course of Western civilization, as well as the story arc of the second season of the *X-Files*. Clearly, you need to know more."

"Do you recall that Gargamel believed that Smurfs could be turned into gold? That was most likely crap, Gargamel having failed sophomore year chemistry and all, demented thinking resulting from improperly ventilated cauldron fumes. Gerald Ford once said the same thing about Granada, so we probably shouldn't put too much stock in it. Still though… what if? Gargamel also thought Smurfs could be made to taste like any of the finest foods on the planet. Surely *something* had to be true, even if not that."

"Admittedly, this build-your-own Smurf kit does not allow you to build any of the named Smurfs you know and love. No Papa Smurf, Handy Smurf, or Smurfette. Not even Brainy. The included equipment instead allows you to make generic Smurfs that may or may not hold one or more generic orange plastic "Smurf" implements. I do not assert anything to the contrary. However, is that not in fact the very advantage of this fine product? Those already existing Smurfs are prima donnas, expensive and unreasonably demanding. Your generic gray clay Smurfs will be grateful to simply exist, willing to do anything in exchange. They will do your bidding without even requiring actual names, much less a craft table of assorted Danish raw fish pastries."

"It's the best of all worlds."

"Now, management does not allow me to promise that your Smurf army will take over the known world and force Ann Coulter to feed you peeled red grapes while wearing a string bikini patterned after the national flag of Angola. At the same time though, they conspicuously did *not* instruct me to promise that the reverse wouldn't happen either. I think we all know what that means, wink-wink, blame the lawyers."

"So, who will be first in line for this marvelous, breakthrough product? It won't be available long. In fact, it's already only for sale at the Target on Saddle Creek circa 1982. Don't let it get any further away from you than that."

"Act now."

Tony Robbins Told Fred to Follow Others' Dreams Instead of His Own Because They Thought Bigger

They say to dress for the job you want rather than the one you have, but I don't know if I've had much luck growing my height to six-foot-four and putting on too-small dark suits. The addition of platform shoes may have helped a bit, but I think putting an "Angus Scrimm residence" sign out front was overboard…even if I did move to a small-town mortuary first.

For some reason, people thought I was a theatrical basketball player. I guess they all equated "tall" with only one thing and anyone not affiliated with the sport could go lump it. I found myself under contract as a villain fighting the team up of the Harlem Globetrotters and Scooby-Doo, despite my inability to even dribble.

I didn't get discouraged though. I built an army of flying chrome spheres that could shoot drills and blades out their fronts, filled them with brains from corpses I then shrunk down into little trolls. No real idea why, but that's what I did. Unfortunately, the trolls kept getting confused for the Sand People from Tatooine. Next thing I knew, I was doing voice-overs for a *Lawrence of Arabia*-themed *Star Wars* amusement park and leaving flaming bags of ocelot excrement on George Lucas' front porch.

It wasn't quite the career path I'd been hoping for.

I imagined the metal balls would have kept things straight more, but they apparently gave the impression I was trying to stump for a pinball machine version of the whole scheme. The Federal Reserve simply explained that arcades weren't too profitable anymore, but promised to keep my idea in mind in case the business landscape changed.

Perhaps I should have been speaking up louder. Repeating "you play a good game, boy" certainly wasn't enough. In fact, I think it reinforced the pinball mistake. Listening to Elton John tunes didn't help my case either.

Of course, eventually they were all part of my army anyway, their husks turned into trolls and their brains floating in my flying metal balls. A whole lot of people died as part of that, let me tell you. Maybe I didn't think that part through, though their mistakes didn't make much of a difference at that point. After all, no one was left alive to employ me…but I did have my less than enviable armies. Still, though I came close with my plan, I still was just not quite who I set out to be.

Try as I might, I was still only a tall-ish man.

Martin Van Buren Always Said It's Not For Kids if You Bring Your Own Booze

My dad said he was taking me to ShowBiz Pizza for my birthday, but I'm pretty sure we went to a strip club instead. I don't remember what the Rock-afire Explosion band members were supposed to be called, but I'm almost positive it wasn't "Candi," "Lucki," "Trixi," and "Loretta." Taking off their clothes didn't seem normal either. I don't know how my dad got them to wear those animal heads if we were somewhere else though.

It seemed odd that the arcade games showed little movies about park rangers and pool cleaners named things like "Dirk" and "Lance." The plots were kind of thin and the lighting was bad, but somehow the tokens I brought from home still worked. Got a lot of tickets too, even if they were only good for wells.

The claw machine wasn't bad, though it might have actually been someone's artificial limb and a lady's purse. Whatever, it was full of thong underwear and dollar bills, smelled a bit like baby powder. There was a bunch of individually wrapped latex as well, though they were rubber surgical gloves, oddly enough. I didn't even want to know about that one.

My dad denied deceit when pressed, but ShowBiz never used to sell microwave pizza rolls and whiskey. They also had plates rather than serving on crumpled sheets of last week's want ads. I wasn't going to complain about the food though, considering it was a step up. For once it didn't have me in the bathroom for hours, which was really good considering all the holes in those stalls.

Though apparently, that made me miss out on something called a "powder party." Oh well, that's probably okay.

The waitress asked if I was a big boy now, but my dad

chased her off. He said he didn't have the money for that, whatever that was supposed to mean. All the other men seemed to have enough, at least enough for a couple times each, so it couldn't have been too much. My dad went to talk to her in private for a while too, but I didn't get anything. I called him on it, but he said I wouldn't like champagne.

And mom would get madder than she was already going to be.

Regardless, ShowBiz parties aren't supposed to end up in the drunk tank, and the girls who work there are often sixteen. No one ever says much about it, the vice squad included. I had dad on that one, but he snuck away to deal with Lenny the Snitch so we'd get in good with the shot caller.

Oh well, Gran still sang me "Happy Birthday" through that glass. I only wish the phone hadn't cut out before she was done. At least she posted bail.

Mind you, it still beat the skate party from the year before. No matter what dad says, I'm pretty sure "skate" isn't spelled "skag" in Norway.

To Kill a Mokkingbird II — Kill Harder by Ahrrper Leeeeee (title courtesy of Jon Konrath)

A dilapidated RV roars out of the sunrise on a deserted highway outside Fresno. CUT to inside the RV's cab: an obviously unwashed Boo Radley is at the wheel, adjusting his elaborately bad comb-over on top of his even worse toupée. *This is going to destroy Carmine*, he thinks in a narrated voice. *He may be taking bribes, but he's a good guy. He's trying to do what's right. I hate it, but there's no choice. Scout and I would never have been involved in this if Jeb hadn't been shot at that gun range by a veteran he was trying to help in order to come to terms with his past as a Navy SEAL sniper in Iraq.*

Suddenly, the RV is hijacked by Dominic Toretto and Dill during a high speed and very flashy street race when Dominic's modified 1970 Dodge Charger (previously owned by his late father) collides with a semi-truck. Dominic asks if Boo "gets the drift" of what the situation is and expects Dill to chuckle. However, Dill only crosses his legs and sips a martini because he's undercover busting Dominic's theft ring to expunge Dill's conviction for smuggling unapproved AIDS treatments across the Mexican border to his buyer's club.

Dominic crashes the RV into a tree and Boo, Scout (wearing one of those 70's disco outfits that show a lot of side boob), and Dill are rescued from the hospital by Atticus, who needs them to pretend to be transforming robots from outer space as part of a CIA operation to sneak hostages out of Iran in the early 80s. Dill tells Atticus: "Argo fuck yourself!" This does not go well. Long story short, everybody but Scout dies.

Left on her own, Scout is forced into an arena where contestants must kill each other to amuse a crowd in order to survive. She's cool with that, but gets a nasty paper cut and is granted a disability pension. While trying to fly home, her old nemesis former U.S. Army Special Forces Colonel Stuart and other members of his unit take control of Scout's plane in an attempt to rescue General Ramon Esperanza. Scout shoots a bunch of people and blows up some stuff, eventually making it home. However, she trips while getting off the plane and realizes she has a rare early-onset slow-progressing form of amyotrophic lateral sclerosis (ALS) that will gradually paralyze her.

Faced with her degenerative condition, Scout devotes herself to unifying the general theory of relativity with quantum mechanics. [Insert robotic voice talking about the universe here.] She falls in love with Jane Wilde, who is devoted to Scout but has difficulty coping with the full extent of Scout's daily needs (particularly given Jane's dreams to build a robotic suit to fight bad guys). Eventually, Scout gets a copy of *Penthouse* and their lives rewind to the moment Scout and Jane met, mirroring Scout's wish to reverse time to see what happened at the beginning of the universe.

As a result, Scout learns a powerful lesson both about not judging people by the color of their skin and about the human tendency to destroy innocence. However, that doesn't do anybody any good because humanity is immediately destroyed when the sun goes supernova, blasting (by a complex and contrived series of events) gigantic zombie SHARKS!!! throughout the galaxy.

Credits roll.

Willy Wonka Spent More Time in OSHA Hearings Than Making Candy

Gene Wilder may be dead now, but at least he won't be hiding jelly beans in my shower anymore. He used to pry up the little ceramic tiles and dig cavities with a shoemaker's awl, placing one bean of any number of various fruit-flavored types before gluing everything down again with industrial-strength contact adhesive.

I'd find a couple every morning while getting ready for work. Rarely, if ever, would I actually make it to breakfast. Just not hungry after that I suppose, and even Wilford Brimley told me I needed to change my eating habits.

What a wakeup call, eh?

I talked to Gene about it one time, after I caught him in that organic silk fishing net I borrowed from Daryl Hannah, but he insisted it was all privileged action as a reference to his famous film. Frankly, I personally didn't see what jelly beans had to do with him starring as a Sherlock Holmes's deaf brother trying to bring Peter Boyle back to life in prison using only a black sheriff and a pair of red satin bikini panties.

What do I know though? I mainly watch talkies.

Using the tub instead of the shower wasn't much help either. That's when he started in with the caramel and Marty Feldman commemorative chafing dishes, and I'm still paying the bills for the dental hygienist. My horoscope steered me wrong before, but that was an entirely different level.

No, Gene's passing was the only way to get it all to stop… that or assisting Gargamel to corner the world jelly bean market using broiled Smurf shoes. If I had it to do over again, perhaps I would have gone the latter route after all, no matter what the impact on the Norwegian rain forests would be.

At the end of the day, we'd at least still have Gene.

MTV Was Originally Supposed to be Targeted at Unmarried Monitor Lizards Before the Red Green PBS Pledge Drive Fell Short and Randy Quaid Ate All the Waffles

If Tom Cochrane doesn't stop backseat driving, I'm going to turn this vintage BMW hovercraft around right now. I'm doing him a solid, driving him from the Des Moines suburbs to downtown Los Angeles so he can have his teeth arthroscopically replaced with *SpongeBob SquarePants* decorative glass anal beads, I don't have to put up with any crap. If I wanted that, I would have given Debbie Harry a ride again.

"Drive faster, cops won't pull anybody in a tan vehicle over for going less than ten times the velocity of light reduced by a constant roughly equivalent to a jar of cactus marmalade over the speed limit unless their price and participation is varying." Seriously, who does this jerk think he is? Does he think I'm some kind of rube?

"Stop setting me on fire. I don't like that." Tough luck, buddy. Lump it. I'm the driver, so I make the rules…and the rules right now say the passenger gets set on fire for the next ten miles unless I get fifty bucks in Camel Cash, so you better cough up or let me focus on driving. You're the one that got in. Well, I did too…but not as a lame-o passenger. I'm not that dumb.

"If science can develop a dog food that makes its own gravy, how come they can't create a sandwich that makes its own potato salad?" Distracting, dude. Studies show that inattentive drivers are worse than motorcyclists who've been freebasing herbal Nembutals with Monica Lewinsky's telegraph operator. You want that on your head along with the fate of that cannibal tribe from Eastern Michigan? I sure wouldn't. Why didn't you ask the important questions when I had cruise control on and hopped a Union Carbide freight train to the Dominican Republic for a quick breather? I had plenty of time to muse then.

Honestly, next time he gets out to play guitar in the middle of the road for a while, I'm taking off and leaving him. I don't have enough of my break left for this.

Man, try to do a guy a favor.

Benjamin Franklin was pissing on my apartment building door

Benjamin Franklin was pissing on my apartment building door when I went out for a smoke the other night (Old Gold mentholated llama hump ultra-king private reserves, in case you're wondering). He wore a purple iridescent vinyl leisure suit with white silver dollar buttons and had coke dust smeared under his nose. "Thank god you're here," he said, zipping up his pants, or whatever you do with vinyl, "your country needs you!"

So I lit a cigarette and said, "Tell me about it, Ben."

"Those bastards down at the Portland DMV and twenty-four-hour disco won't give me a drink," he wailed, wiping at plutonium riddled sweat trapped in his forehead wrinkles with a soda-sticky sleeve. "Said my money's no good!" I reminded him he was, after all, dead, but he screamed, "My picture is on it for Christ sake!" before a coughing fit shot special interest farm subsidy bills out in his founding father phlegm. They writhed around on the sidewalk looking for deep Szechwan-flavored pockets.

So I lit a cigarette and said, "Tell me about it, Ben."

"How 'bout her," he leered a pork-fat-tinged Ron Jeremy grin at an Alabamanian part-time crack whore chopping up lines of Drano and used laptop batteries on a rancid Wendy's cheeseburger patty, chunky-style vomit encrusted in the curls of her Ogilvie home perm. She smiled at the attention, the vomit apparently hers even if the occasional teeth weren't. "I like her because she's trashy," he said, "and because she's got three Ph.D's. "She's getting me back into politics, or at least coaching Little League. Her dad used to whack Orientals for the Kennedy Administration and her mom, in between tricks, heads the local DAR."

So I lit a cigarette and said, "Tell me about it, Ben."

Then he grabbed me by the shoulders in his majestic

turkey waddle hands, dripping second amendments on my good fake tuxedo T-shirt, and leaned in like it was tax time. "Listen," he said, "you gotta help me out. We're driving all night to Michigan and we need gas money." But all my cash had gone for jelly beans and Mr. Clean Magic Erasers, so he told me Uncle Sam would pork barrel me up-against-the-wall when the Nicaraguan two-for-one polyester revolution came.

So I lit a cigarette and said, "Tell me about it, Ben."

But he'd already jacked a North Vegas ambulance and pizza delivery panel truck to film documentaries on the history of failed silk work separatist movements at the North Pole, so I put out my cigarettes and went back inside. I even peed on the door a little myself, in case you're wondering.

Some Joker Labeled All Medicare Forms Ultra-Classified Burn Before Reading and Then the Entire Country Other Than Sloth From *Goonies* Was in the Dark From Then On

Wanted: One Econoline Camping Trailer, powder blue… though it isn't for me ma.

Willing to pay top dollar for decent condition, and/or if used by famous pirates to hide buried treasure in the suburbs of Houston. Serious inquiries only, and/or lonely members of the Bull Moose Party who want to talk to someone, because I need to buy ASAP.

Up to $10K for the right model, or a combination of money, easy credit rip-off terms, and/or bodily organs (for either the product or purchase price).

Not that I really need to put this in the ad, but I'm going to set out this summer to find America while I've got time off from stealing Charmin toilet paper from Mormons for Walmart. Not the metaphor for hopes and dreams and a fair chance to earn a basic living and succeed that everyone is always blathering on about, I'm looking for a Midwestern truck stop where I blacked out on Mini Thins one time when jumping bail on a charge of aiding and abetting the Roaring Twenties corruption of J. Edgar Hoover's pug dog Francis. Totally a frame job by Oscar Mayer, but I think the stop was called Little America or something. I remember a penguin being involved.

I might have left my original 1974 Japanese release Hello Kitty plastic coin purse stuffed full of prescription narcotic multivitamins in the women's bathroom.

Anyway, none of that is really your business. Just let me know if you have a trailer or not, preferably one you'd be willing to sell or admit you don't keep a good enough eye on when you park it at your mother-in-law's frosting factory. I do want the trailer-only model rather than one of the full RV jobs as I plan to take my boss's two-tone racing Vespa along with me. He doesn't really know, so don't tell him because I want it to be a surprise.

Warren Beatty loves surprises.

Vespas can tow a couple thousand pounds of pornographic *Space Ghost* collectible silver half dollar coins, right?

Also, I would like to sell one complete collection of ballpark hot dogs partially eaten by significant Yankees infielders of the eighties. I don't want to get rid of these, but I've got to finance this trailer ad somehow. Classifieds charge by the word and I don't see how to make this any more concise.

Sally Field has a Penchant for Bare-Knuckle Boxing When Filming Romances and Producers Have to Factor in Bribes to the John Birch Society Accordingly When Budgeting New Projects

I weighed over seven thousand pounds when I bought that warehouse in the rough part of Shawnee Mission Parkway. I had to, nowhere else had enough space. My body wasn't overweight by any means, muscle-bound if anything, but I was eighty feet tall.

Strangely, the two numbers had no relation.

Don't you remember your parents telling you to eat that frozen spinach when you were a kid so you'd grow big and strong? Yeah, apparently, I'm the only sucker who bought it. Now I'm the size of a Tyrannosaurus and Randy from third-period gym won't stop calling to ask if Booger Jones has returned from his stripper glitter prospecting trip to the Pyrenees.

So now I live in a warehouse.

It's not as bad as one might think. Plenty of space, if nothing else. It's also a great investment. Strange asexual animal beings that burn the air when they talk and are perpetually shadowed because light seems afraid of them keep making increasingly higher, worseningly desperate, and progressively more threatening offers for the place. That's a good thing, right? I'm still waiting for all that to catch up on Zillow, and for someone to waive inspection.

There was that trouble with the symphonic zoning board, but absent robotic parts, dinosaur DNA, radiation poisoning, or laser beams, the Monster Island statutes simply don't apply to me. I'm big, but I'm human…even if I can beat the Arnold Clark Studio photographers in a nuclear-arms wrestling tables, ladders, and chairs (when they aren't cheating) match. Also, they allowed residential use the moment that fast-talking developer got that variance to convert the Pepsi Center to high-priced fish condos.

It's a done deal now.

So here I am in my little, cozy warehouse, bought and paid for. Gamera is coming over to watch the Mariners game in thirty minutes while Mothra and George Stephanopoulos wax my ATV.

All in all, it's not a bad life.

Better Wash Really Good if Someone is Going to be Touching Your Flyback Anode

I'm ashamed to admit that I was no less prejudiced against the robots when they were first introduced to society than anyone else, including Ed Meese. How could I not be with Robert Loggia filing my head with all that claptrap about them stealing our farm subsidies and raping our city council ombudsmen? I know better now, but that doesn't make up for some of the things I've done, or the fried chicken I've eaten. None of us. Like the manager of the 16th Street Mall Radio Shack, we all have reasons not to be proud.

The military models were fine, none of us other than Linda Hamilton ever saw those, but I didn't know what about the anniversary release of that *They Live* DVD box set/ blue cheese-dipped finger sandwich bundle made Universal Studios think people wanted robots in everyday life. The first one I met was a Jiggle Belly Santa, stationed during the holidays in the lobby of my office building.

It was worse than when Nicolas Cage used to beg for spare change and pocket lint in the parking lot.

Seriously, he'd stand there motionless until someone walked by and then suddenly start gyrating and singing. It was awful, just like when Wendell Willkie directed the ballet. "Santa Claus is Coming to Town" would play over and over again when traffic through the lobby was heavy. Why have him dance? It was like those damn flopping fish that sang N.W.A. songs. This was an office, not a Spencers Gifts outlet.

We got so sick of Jiggle Belly Santa that we started unplugging him despite the razor wire placed there to prevent precisely that. Building management kept plugging him right back in, so we coated the plug contacts with clear nail polish and dogfish oil. That fooled them for a bit, but then they simply hardwired the robot into the main power grid of the building. It started not a few fires, and it was embarrassing. We all started using the back entrance, even with all the motion-activated turret guns. Certainly, no one was going to send clients through the main lobby.

I guess building management finally caved after the midnight riots. One day, Jiggle Belly Santa was gone, fired. I didn't see him again until I found him working on the counter at a porn store in New Jersey. The stripping was pathetic enough, but the paid sex acts were heartrending. Of course, it wasn't as if the store could officially peddle his robot behind for money…but everyone knew that was part of the deal if he wanted to keep his job. What do you think Betamax stands for?

I guess that was the only work he could get.

Then I started feeling bad about how we'd treated Jiggle Belly Santa. I mean, if we'd known he was willing to do that kind of stuff we'd have never forced him from the building.

It's downright inconvenient to have to drive to Jersey all the time.

Kidnapping with Margaret Thatcher

The first time that Margaret Thatcher kidnapped me, it was sometime in the very beginning of the eighties. I'm pretty sure it was around when Reagan traded packets of honey-roasted peanuts to the rioting air traffic controllers for the *CBS Storybreak* hostages. Either way, the whole thing was a mistake — at least as much on my part as it was hers.

I mean, I knew I shouldn't have picked up that savings and loan off the sidewalk. Sure, it looked new, but germs weren't the only concern. At that point, Ivan Boesky was still on death row in Mississippi for lacing derivative vehicles with cyanide. Also, it wasn't as if I hadn't picked up various banking corporations off the street before only to wake up in a motel bathtub full of ice with either a kidney removed or added.

Sure enough, not long after picking it up, my vision started to go dark and I thought: *Great, I wonder if I'll gain or lose a kidney this time.* Honestly, I was having trouble keeping track of exactly how many kidneys I might or might not have had in there. Spring forward, fall back onto the dialysis table and all that, but I could have had dozens, or none, for all I knew.

But, it was a bit different when I came to that time. For one thing, I'd never had my illicit kidney harvestings/implantations done in a unisex bathroom in the basement of Paddington Station. For another, I'd never been dressed in a neon pink vinyl tutu and had my toenails painted lime green while trussed up like a turkey in bailing wire. That really was a new direction — both for me and for all of England.

"So," Margaret Thatcher spoke pleasantly, cracking an electrified horse-whip, "I hear you don't care for strong women."

"Actually, Ma'am, that's not really true," I responded. "Besides, I think *Bloom County* already did this bit."

Margaret looked puzzled for a moment. That didn't really work for her, dressed as she was in an all-black leather and steel version of Evel Knievel's uniform.

Mind you, you're probably thinking some kind of dominatrix thing here, and that couldn't be further from the case. Margaret was absolutely professional; there was nothing sexual about it. I've seen few things less sexual, and keep in mind that I sat through the entirety of *Eyes Wide Shut*.

"What? Aren't you Mr. Val Kilmer?" Margaret asked in a stern, yet almost matronly way.

"No, Ma'am. My name's Chuck. I'm a dental phrenologist."

Margaret rolled her eyes and gave the nearby loo a light kick with one of her black jackboots. Of course, the tips of her toes were covered in heavy, polished steel spikes and the porcelain shattered instantly to powder.

"Honestly," she muttered. "How is one expected to run a civilized country when one's underlings are utter incompetents? This one doesn't even *look* like Mr. Kilmer."

"Sorry, Ma'am," I spoke up. "I'm sure you're doing your very best."

She smiled. "You are a sweet child," she told me. "Would you mind terribly if I tortured you anyway? We are both here already and everything."

I said I didn't mind. I was relatively comfortable where I was, after all, and Annette Funicello's *How Will I Know My Love* was playing over the station's PA system. A couple hours of torture wasn't going to ruin my day.

Anyway, Margaret Thatcher went ahead and twisted my arms in their sockets until I screamed. Then she made me eat an entire copy of *The Poorly Illustrated Works of Charles Dickens* before pulling out my fingernails and having me recite the alphabet backward.

It was certainly painful, but I'll hand it to Margaret that she was well organized. She'd already managed to re-insert all of my fingernails by the time I woke up in that dumpster outside the Waffle House in Miami.

*

Now, I don't think anyone could possibly blame me in any way for the second time Margaret Thatcher kidnapped me. After all, who wouldn't enter a *Max Headroom* personal full-body electroplating contest sponsored by M. Thatcher Enterprises? It was billed as "So much fun, it's torture!" Heck, I would have been a fool to pass that one up.

Of course, when I woke up in a stock room behind the baggage retrieval system at Heathrow Airport and saw Margaret Thatcher coming at me with a jar of leeches and an entire briefcase full of knock-off Swatches, I'd changed my mind considerably. Still, keep calm and carry on, right?

"Sorry, dearie," she told me while forcing me to narrate the entire first season of *Scarecrow and Mrs. King*, "but this Falklands thing has me a bit tense. I really need to unwind, even if you aren't an enemy of the crown…or even an English subject.

All in all, it wasn't too bad — though I'd never be able to look at mayonnaise and lottery tickets the same way again. At least she didn't do anything like call fries "chips" while the ordeal was ongoing.

*

Mind you, Margaret Thatcher didn't torture me EVERY time she kidnapped me. Why, the third time she just made me dinner. Well, she at least brought me burgers from In-N-Out.

Really, I don't even remember how she kidnapped me that time. One moment I was watching the Obama/ McCain election results rolling in at home while sculpting raspberry Zingers into scenes from various Burt Reynolds/ Dom DeLuise movies, and the next I was crucified to my tile kitchen backsplash by plastic zip ties and electrical tape.

"Hello, Margaret," I said once I realized what was going on, even before I'd opened my eyes.

"Hullo, dear," she responded as she set my kitchen table for our feast of fast food and Schlitz Malt Liquor. "I thought it was time to stop by and remind you that I'm still in charge, even if I'm not prime minister anymore."

"Don't kid me, Margaret." I shook my head. "I knew that already, what with all the newspaper death threats and locking of everyone I've ever gotten close to in the Tower of London."

She smiled sheepishly, or at least as sheepish as Margaret Thatcher ever looked. "Got me on that one, dear," she admitted. "I guess I just missed you. One does get a bit lonely from time to time being the Iron Lady."

And it was nice, no pain at all. It would have been one of the best evenings I'd had in years if she hadn't torched my house while I was still tied to my kitchen wall.

To this day, I'm still not sure I could say what all the kidnapping meant. Who can say what anything means? Margaret Thatcher could, but she's passed on. The age of iron is definitely over. Today is bronze at best.

Honestly, I don't think the news has fully set in. I mean, the next time my kneecaps get broken with a polo mallet, it will be by someone else. The next time someone holds my head underwater and punches me in the stomach, it won't be Margaret Thatcher. I could always get snatched again, but never more will I be kidnapped by her. Honestly, when it finally hits me, I think I'll be a little bit sad.

Could anyone even imagine being abducted by Tony Blair? What would be the point in that?

I Got A Lot Less Cavities Once I Started Gargling Daily With Hydrogenated Mechanic's Lye, But the Bleeding Was Awkward at Bachelor Parties

Once upon a time, Gerald Ford was president. He was a good president and was very happy. However, then his electorate died in a freak Magnavox metal acoustic breakfast sausage band saw accident and Gerald Ford's father married a new, evil electorate for him. This made Gerald Ford very unhappy.

It made Gerald Ford so unhappy because the evil electorate wanted to get rid of him and replace him with an android party sheep made in Japan. The evil electorate would do bad things to Gerald Ford, like override his vetoes or make him do all the White House chores with no help. It even would send him to the Lincoln Bedroom without supper after making him vacuum the Oval Office, particularly under the furniture.

Gerald Ford was the saddest president ever.

But then one day, things got worse. The evil electorate sent Gerald Ford to Grandma Wolf's Pumpkin Ball in the woods at the Three Bear's gingerbread cottage. His shoes didn't fit, so he had to stuff them with breadcrumbs because an old flying witch ate all of his golden pebbles. On his way, Gerald Ford was kidnaped by a lonely, cursed princess who would turn into a horrific beast if someone would kiss a boot-wearing frog, but Gerald only wanted to be friends.

All kinds of bad shit happened.

Long story short, Gerald Ford killed all of the dentists using his shoes and a magic thimble he found in a hollow tree. Fearing Hague prosecution for dental-based war crimes,

Gerald asked his fairy Jimmy Carter for help. Luckily, Jimmy could make anything cool.

That's just what Jimmy did.

So, Jimmy told Gerald Ford to switch clothes with him and fork over some peanuts and Jimmy would become president in his place. Gerald complied and went into hiding by taking a job in the Mark Twain Hydraulic Things That Look Suspiciously Like Sex Toys Museum while Jimmy faced the heat, and the nation.

Turns out it wasn't a big deal after all though because no one liked dentists.

Free Ball Cap Day at the Indiana State Penitentiary Hasn't Helped Recidivism

You know, I don't think you people appreciate the true value of hats. If you did, you'd be running out to buy some right now at Circuit City or Bergdorf Goodman instead of asking me questions like "what am I doing at two a.m. in this modern art museum loading a furry toilet into a Styrofoam packing crate" and "why am I not wearing any pants." None of that matters when there are hats to consider.

Without William the Orange waving his hat, there never would have been an end to the War of the Roses, the movie or the historical event. Many of you think William the Orange wasn't involved in the War of the Roses, but that's only because he was disguised by his hat. You didn't recognize him. That hat wave, along with a timely text message, is what made Northumberland not come to the aid of King Richard. Northumberland had a powerful fear of hats, just like most drugstore junkies.

I know you've all heard a different story, but that's only anti-hat propaganda. Joseph McCarthy was big on that.

Jesus used hats to walk across the sea of never-ending pasta at the Cincinnati Olive Garden. He just strapped them to his feet like ducks and off he went. It's true that the hats were lined with inflatable sheep bladders from his secret crime-fighting dirigible, but I don't think that diminishes the contribution of the hats. Apostle Creed didn't think so either, otherwise, he wouldn't have spent thirty years living as a hermit in the hats afterward — one on odd numbered days and the other on alternate evens.

Hats are something you could put the Ark of the Covenant in. Then people would be all like: *Shit! You found the Ark of the Covenant! It's in that hat you've got there!*

With the right hat, you can turn people to good or evil. Cowboy directors used to do it all the time, though only in moderation. They simply had to remember to swap all the black hats for white when the actors died. Otherwise, they'd be responsible for sending all those souls to hell. Equity frowns on that, and repeated violations can get one permanently barred from the craft services table. No director wants that.

Don't you know the role of hats in the history of the CIA? Ever heard of keeping something under your hat? That refers to how Nikolai Tesla used to kill double agents by stuffing a fedora down their throats so they couldn't call out to the flock of Graham Greene impersonators for help. He was always getting his hair full of saliva, but no one did more for America. That's also how he discovered static cling. He'd have been up a creek without that hat, or his lucky overshoes.

No, I think you people need to stop and reconsider hats thoroughly right now. That'd be a much more productive use of your time than arresting me for grand theft and indecency. Trust me.

Would I lie to you?

Kim Jong-un Has to Sit at the Kid's Table Because He Kept Trying to Annex the Gravy

We'd never missed a Thanksgiving celebration before, but the Paris trip made things difficult. The French had a weird way of observing the day, pretending they weren't doing anything at all, almost like it wasn't even a holiday. We weren't buying that. Never trust the French.

It certainly wasn't what we were used to.

So, I decided to make my own Thanksgiving right there in the hotel room. My tools were limited, but I had plenty of bears. Well, I was sure I had at least one. Surely that was enough. Ernest Borgnine had less to work with when he fought off the Shōgun's troops singlehandedly at the battle of Bunker Hill using only a BeDazzler, seven Ginsu knives, and a crate of smokeless ashtrays.

I could do this.

The closest thing I had to a turkey was a rubber chicken from my Groucho Marx disguise. The closest to stuffing was a wad of already chewed garlic-flavored novelty gum. Cooking facilities were lacking as well. What we had was an electric kettle provided by the hotel to boil water for instant coffee and discount ramen noodles. It wasn't much, but this was a day to be grateful.

I needed to count my blessings and think of all I did have, like Brendan Fraser in *Encino Man*.

So, I popped up some popcorn and grilled a few slices of toast. It may not have been traditional, but we were all together. That was what was important, not eel flavored cranberry jelly and olive stuffed pumpkin pie. Who cares if we didn't have Cognac-candied turkey livers and deviled marshmallow fluff salad? We felt pretty good about our efforts until Peppermint Patty called shenanigans on the whole deal, but then that worked out too when we reminded her of the real spirit behind the day.

Wait…no, that's not right. That was *A Charlie Brown Thanksgiving*, not what we did. Can't see how I got those two mixed up. We didn't even watch that cartoon. The hotel's Wi-Fi was a little slow.

The boiled garlic rubber chicken we'd cooked by filling it from the electric teakettle in the shower wasn't bad though. The hand-soap carvings made lousy mashed potatoes, but how often do the real ones come out right anyway? We'd certainly had worse Thanksgiving dinners, what with that family recipe for salmonella green bean casserole, though not by a huge margin.

I just hope that our vacation to the missile fields of North Korea this summer doesn't yield similar problems for Independence Day. One strained holiday a year is enough.

Just ask Alfred Dreyfus.

Michael Rennie was There the Day I Forgot my Bus Pass, But He Told Me Which Metro Line Went to the Ziegfeld Follies

The day after the apocalypse turned out to be somewhat of a letdown. Target wasn't even running a sale and we had to wait in a fairly decent-sized line to stock up on the limited-edition anchovy-flavored Cheez-Its. Steven Wright was running around in vanilla pudding filled galoshes smacking pedestrians with a stuffed emperor penguin, so it was all pretty much business as usual.

There weren't even any less people on the road to the eighty-seventh Republican presidential debate and used plastic humidor flea market.

It probably made a difference that nothing had really happened, no zombie epidemic, no everyone plugging in their Dyson home rototilling vacuum cleaner and combination fish dehydrators at the same time. We'd simply decided to finally make November 26th the apocalypse so we could stop trying to predict the day it would come. Thus, the 27th was the day after. It was largely a paper thing, but it sufficed.

Finally, something on the national agenda that transcended partisan rancor.

It was weird though that no one was gone. One expected the day after to have empty streets, crumpled paper and used aluminum pantyhose blowing everywhere. Martin Sheen introduced a bill that would require two-fifths of the population to stay home on any given day to keep up the traditional conception, but that didn't go very far when people remembered he didn't really hold political office. The same went for Isaac Hayes.

It's so hard to remember that sometimes.

Theft became a problem for a bit. After all, what's to stop people from taking whatever they want once the apocalypse occurs? Well, the police, EAS Anti-Shoplifting Security System Products, Boss Hogg, pajama-bearing Muscovites dedicated to social justice after misreading the secret seventh chapter of *Charlotte's Web*, and so on. In short, everything that normally stopped people on every day before the 26th.

People kept overlooking that the apocalypse was only strictly an observance.

One kooky group of athletically-inclined income tax adjusters in East Lansing got really hammered on poster paint fumes and low-fat bacon and tried to prognosticate that the world was going to end in a week due to invasion by sentient dancing silkworms from outer space, but everyone just laughed and they got real embarrassed. It was so hard on that sort to have to be constantly reminded that they were too late for doomsday predictions.

Thanks, Obama.

The worst was having to still go to work. It was like getting to the afterlife and finding out that Heaven was actually *Belle and Sebastian* reruns with John Stamos voicing Poochie. Thankfully I'd just gotten that job surgically replacing Folgers Crystals in the jars on Macy's store shelves with radioactive Cadbury Creme Eggs. At least that somewhat made up for it.

Which was good, since federal law mandated that I feel fine regardless.

If I Were Tom Hanks, I Would have Just Gotten the Klopeks to Sponsor my Application to Live at the Vatican so I Could go Back to Work Designing Toys as Soon as Possible

I went and hung out on some designer folding chairs at the airport today. Not that I had a flight, preferring transubstantiation to air travel as I did, I just wanted to be seen. Airports were such status symbols anymore. Second only would be the bus station, but with as many times as Norm Macdonald stabbed people for bacon-flavored meth money, why risk it? Just go for the airport, especially since that puts you higher up on the society page anyways.

Right below waterless plumbers.

Sure, airports had become a bit less welcoming since Amelia Earhart stole the entire United fleet, taking it to Belarus to get the deposit money for renting video tapes. After that, you couldn't get through security unless you were the one flying the plane and had immediate male family members still in the country for the airlines to raffle off as circus performers in case you pulled a runner. Still, people could at least sit by ticketing, as long as the seating was in an impermanent configuration, presuming they didn't mind getting mugged by rogue flight attendants for 20-ounce bottles of Sunny Delight once an hour or so.

Most thought the hassle worth it.

Though, few wanted to actually fly anymore. Once they went to random postmodernist destinations as opposed to fixed flight paths in an attempt to confused Boutros Boutros-

Ghali, it wasn't as an efficient mode of transportation as it used to be. Most couldn't afford it either, what with all fares being payable only in solid gold and amounting to the average net cost of five Nabisco Oreo ice cream factories.

It just didn't make sense for American families.

I managed to get seen though, sitting there in my hard-won chair. They even took my picture for the paper and my fingerprints for that Federal United Volleyball Association doughnut registry. It was cool; I talked to Warren Buffet there while all that was going on. He asked to borrow five bucks and a bucket of fried chicken.

Rich guys got hungrier than normal people.

Of course, the airport might not let me hang out there much longer, I figured. Someone put together that my wife was the one packing my briefcase every morning and it seemed I got on some kind of list. I didn't know what the FAA was going to do about it, but my name was right between the quart of camel milk and the dozen farm-fresh goat eggs.

That was disconcerting, to say the least.

They're Your Fears, They're Your Terrors and They Live in a Cave in the Pit of Your Psyche and All are Named John Jacob Jingleheimer Schmidt

It's funny, but my takeover of the world started when I tried to get my old girlfriend back. Strange how often people say that, but it's true. She'd left after I sold her kidneys to the Labor movement to get spare cash to rent *Snow Dogs* on VHS, so I knew I needed a real 80s gesture to get her back and scrawled "Sarah, come back I love you" in chalk on the sidewalk outside her work. Only problem was she worked at Grand Central Station, one of the busiest train centers in the world.

Lot of Sarahs go by there.

Do you know how many showed up at my house? Including a last name might have been smart, or even some mention of my name for reference. Sarah Jessica Parker and Sarah Michelle Gellar drove together, though they made Sarah Palin take a bus. Sarah Silverman claimed she never left me in the first place, though Sarah Winnemucca cast some aspersions on that. Sarah Bernhardt projected from beyond the grave, though Sarah Polk simply showed up in her body despite being over a hundred years dead. My apartment was crowded AF, and was getting a bit confusing.

What was I to do?

I mean, it was entirely possible my Sarah might have been in that mass somewhere, but there was no real way to tell short of a recall election. I tried to take a straw man poll, but gave up after they voted in the eighth straw man. No, something else was needed…something flame-broiled.

Instead, I got the idea to write "Sarah, capture the Rhineland" on the flagstones outside. Luckily, I still had that chalk...and could still get out the door. *Boom*! Quick as a flash, my apartment was empty again...and my domination campaign had its first land gain. Of course, my Sarah, if she'd been there at all, was long gone as well.

My plan had a few holes.

But I made do with what I had, like any good American luxury ice cream truck mechanic with an army of Sarahs would. If I couldn't have my old girlfriend back, I could at least have the world. And, contrary to what that James Bond phony would tell you, though that's his worst movie besides *James Bond Makes Breakfast for the Soccer-Curious Martians,* the world is enough.

At least, it is for me.

I contemplate the humble potato

I sit in my air-conditioned box suite at Madison Square Garden and contemplate the humble potato, that ambitious squishy sack of malevolent grub-like tuberousness as if my life depended on it…for it very well may.

The potato, that murderous sneak who pursued me here hidden in the provided sporting arena concessions. Chips, wedges, even potato matter concealed in flour buns. Pursued me no doubt in attempt to catch me unaware and extinguish my life.

My time is better spent contemplating the potato than the lobster. That ineffectual crustacean merely rattles its chitinous plates on the local news in outrage over power plant closings and socialist runs for city council positions, claims Fischer Price and Tonka have sold out America in exchange for Polident bond futures.

No, the potato is the imminent danger–with its overpriced organic schemings and plottings, directing from the tangible dark humanity's overthrow.

Its maggoty vacuum hose tentacles: the ones that probe from the burlap dusty lower places, fixing midterm elections and toddler beauty pageants with secret B movie mad scientist intelligence. I'm reminded of the deep-throated reverb maniacal laughter of elephants in the Kansas City Zoo.

The potato rots its oily blacky ooze, decomposing Nebraskan whole wheat Vaseline slickyness, which metastasizes and mortalizes all deep-fried Crisco foodstuffs from deep within its lair in a Masonic plywood kitchen cupboard.

I contemplate its aid to wintertime high-octane slug collectors and obese bellybutton thieves, mortal enemies of man. The potato, kin to telemarketing rasping demons that dwell in the cotton candy-filled wastelands where circumcised cowboy clowns once carved betel nut husks into dimes. Elders of russet filth, gnomes of Trinity College term-end report cards, Velveeta foil wrappers of crinkling Sundays.

I feel sour milk nightmare on my dehydrated, starchy tongue and know the menace hiding below Flagstaff and deep within the antediluvian mud temple of synchronous sin in Idaho.

So, in league with Ron Popeil and his circular Bedouin empire of porcelain welfare cheats (both my current Madison Square Garden box suite guests and immediate assistants in destroying the starchy assassins via consumption-oriented mastication), I contemplate the humble potato…and its unquenchable powdered SlimFast drive for murder.

I only hope it isn't too late.

The Tour Boat Narration was so Bad That I had No Choice But to Set Them All On Fire and Move to Phoenix to Study Shiatsu Dog Massage

My hotel bathtub wouldn't drain once I'd filled it all the way for my soak, so I decided to say "fuck it" and become King Neptune. I cranked the water full blast and let it run over the side, flooding a small lake into my room. It was pretty sweet, even if it did knock out the lights and start a small fire.

Benito Mussolini was totes jealous.

Mind you, I needed more than an inland sea for my new role. I wasn't going to do things by half measures, not me. I fashioned a trident from the toilet brush and a crown from the seat. Luckily, I could reach both from where I sat in the tub. After what happened to those poor acrobatic equestrian clowns on the Oregon Trail, I wasn't getting out for anything short of a new expedition to location the Chili's in downtown Boston.

There wouldn't be one of those again for a while, not in this economy.

Of course, the hotel got a bit upset. For one thing, I was flooding the rooms below pretty bad. Also, the manager had already declared himself Neptune while drunk on expired low-fat eggnog at the official Christmas party in March the week before and wasn't looking forward to the competition. That jerk pretender didn't scare me though, the electrified water from the lake hitting the electrical sockets meant he couldn't even enter my room.

Some king of the sea.

Honestly, I'm not sure why the zap didn't fry me too. I

mean, I was in the tub with the same water that juiced him every time he set a foot in or criticized the liberal government of Peru. Why wasn't I getting jolted as well? It was a mystery, just like why I wore that rubber diving suit when bathing.

There were so many puzzles in life.

It seemed as if my reign would be brief, what with my stay only booked for the week and all, but some things were difficult to foresee…like the hotel having checkout policies that specifically excluded asserted divinity. They simply had nothing they could do about me, just like Pete and Pete off that Nickelodeon show, their fault for hiring Captain Nemo to do their legal contract work.

Me? At that point, I was set.

James Garner is Lying if he Says he's With the Band

I was already awake when a blizzard canceled school back in 1982, so I took my combination plastic magnifying glass and Nerf sword cane to look for secret passages and hidden mine shafts in my basement. There weren't any I found after looking for a few minutes, so I opened an all-night disco club instead. The black and white checkered Bakelite squares covering the floor down there made that seem a natural choice, and I had all those hippy records my parents had stacked up.

Lighting was a bit of a problem since I had no disco ball and the seventies were dead as…well, disco, but luckily the wiring was kind of shoddy anyway. The ceiling bulbs already flickered and the additional load from the stereo ended up timing them to the music.

I guessed that was all you needed for a pretty banging disco club.

People came too, blizzard be damned. They'd been starved for a new place since 1980 hit and I pretty much had the market cornered. It wasn't a big market, just one of those little places that sold dusty bottles of soda and dirty magazines in German that hadn't been published in twenty years, but the federal disco assistance subsidies were enough to keep me afloat. Thank god for the National Endowment for the Disco Arts, and for James Woods. That club was a happening place, at least as happening as any other disco club in a kid's basement in 1982.

Of course, maybe all those people showed up simply because they didn't have to go to school that day. That seems unlikely though since they were all in their mid-forties. Admittedly, disco people do age differently than everyone else. Jane Goodall studied that while hanging out with those pizza chimps in the casinos on the French Riviera.

Ivan Boesky's overdose on cocaine and licorice whip-flavored jelly beans put a bit of a damper on the party. Some people just can't handle their sugar. If Steve Martin hadn't hustled him out of there so fast I might have gotten shut down, protection money paid to the Institute of Electrical and Electronics Engineers notwithstanding, but it all thankfully worked out. Steve said they had another party to go to anyway, so he might as well.

I sometimes wonder if Ivan lived.

A massive ICEE cone and nipple waxing conglomerate ended up confiscating the snow in the middle of the night as part of stocking up for next summer's College World Series concession, so school was back on the next day. That was kind of it for the club, sorry to say. It's hard to run something like that from a desk in an elementary school classroom, what with all the decorum one has to maintain there. I was cool with that though.

I had fractions to get to.

It's Not a Feature if the Orange Juice Makes it all Sticky

Life has certainly been interesting since I lost the rights to the color orange in that custody dispute with Humphrey Bogart. I've resorted to dying my carrot sticks green and thank my stars that the airports no longer use that color wheel.

Damn thing was always orange and I wouldn't have ever been able to fly to Reno.

Sure, I secured use of the word "squishy" through the proceedings, but I doubt Bogie had much use for that anyway. It's not his sort of thing, not that orange really is either. He spends most of his time in black and white, Turnerization notwithstanding. I suppose I do get pretty good use out of "squishy," so it's not all bad.

Still, I sure could use the color orange from time to time.

I mean, I've been shot hunting seven times in the last month alone, and that was all just from Easter egg hunts. Lord knows what would have happened if I'd been out looking for deer. Maybe I shouldn't hang out with Dick Cheney so much, or start looking for work outside the legal profession.

That's not even considering Halloween. Couldn't have a pumpkin, had to carve myself a jicama instead. Really started to stink after a bit, and I dulled a hell of a lot of knives in the process. Wasn't very festive either, and I don't think that jack-o'-lantern impressed either Satan or Florence Henderson.

Thank goodness the pie turned out brown instead of orange. I didn't have to resort to any of my fancy tricks there.

Bogie really stuck it to me good with that orange thing. I suppose I shouldn't have followed him around all the time calling him Blue Falcon while pretending to be a comic relief clumsy robotic dog. He hated that, but I couldn't resist. He'd never stop screaming that the reference had nothing to do with his movie, though he knew I knew that.

Also, didn't like it when I got one of them kind of dogs for his AA birthday. He's allergic anyway.

My lawyer thinks we have a chance at an appeal though. He says I can use anything that's a mix of yellow and red because that's a mix of yellow and red and not orange. I said I thought that was merely semantics, but he replied that the law was nothing but semantics.

I don't know, personally. Plastic explosives seem kind of a dangerous thing to resort to over a color, and Semtex-H is often orangish anyway.

Jamming with the Departed Requires a 45 Insert Adapter

People try a lot of different things to talk to the dead: Ouija boards, séances, autonomic writing, used analog Nokia flip phones from the nineties, whatever. Personally, I stick with an old Arthur Brown "Fire" 45 set at 78 RPMs so it sounds like Alvin and the Chipmunks on acid.

It's great. I put it on my "Scooby-Doo Meets Adam Smith's Invisible Hand" Bakelite plastic Victrola and crank away. Quicker than you can say "In my younger and more vulnerable years my father gave me some advice that I've been turning over in my mind ever since," the political career of Bozo the Clown starts speaking to me…usually something about how Guam should reenact the Magellan expedition using dominoes and mushed up Swiss cake rolls.

He's a bit of a card he is.

Now, I know what you're thinking. You're thinking Bozo the Clown didn't have a political career. You'd be right too, at least after that incident involving Alan Greenspan and the Grand Prize Game. Ping pong balls everywhere, and they never could get all the blood out. Steve Guttenberg still has nightmares. No, Bozo's chances for county commissioner out of Bentonville, Arkansas were dead as a doornail that day… just like those poor shaved llamas.

But it still talks, at least when I play that record. I think it just speaks to drown out the song. It always was more of a Lawrence Welk fan, that and Björk. Technically, playing the 45 at 78 RPMs isn't necessary. It'll talk either way. I just keep getting a jolt out of it, and it keeps Dom DeLuise from showing up to perform *Henry VIII* in mime.

That guy can be such a pest.

The record has "The Crazy World of Arthur Brown" on the other side, but I tend to stick to "Fire." The former won't get any ghostly talking going, and I'm sick of causing all those

Knight Rider spinoffs. The one with Robert Mapplethorpe and Desi Arnaz riding around in that synthetic bumper car was just awful.

The "Fire" side is a good deal though. People pay a lot of money to talk to those who've passed on like that, even if rights to the flapjack fortune were already clearly specified in the will. However, I kind of wish I'd get to hear the song. With all that talking, I've never been able to give it a good listen.

There's always something though.

Linseed Oil is Not an Effective Sunblock Ointment Even if You Mix it With Two Parts Crisco and Three Parts Heavy Water Beforehand, James Madison's Amateur Home Hobbyist Chemistry Thesis Notwithstanding

My old elementary school sent out an email about a choose-your-own-peanut-butter fundraiser last week because they were apparently running out of floors. Kids had to stick close to the walls in the hallways and jump a great deal. There had been quite a few falls. The school was starting to worry about legal liability, but there was nothing in the budget for floor replacement. Hardwood is expensive.

I supposed I was at least partially responsible. I mean, I was the one cutting sections out of the floors.

It all started when I used to get distracted in class. Those old boards in the floor formed shapes in my head, what with the seams between planks, the different color stain irregularities, and the lines drawn by Denzel Washington in permanent marker. When I'd see an outline that I recognized, I thought about cutting it out with a chainsaw and using it for something. During school these remained mere thoughts, but let me tell you a fact about adult life: The Home Depot sells chainsaws on credit.

That alone was a game-changer.

What else would anyone have done at that point? As

Deepak Chopra always told everyone to do, I got an 18-inch Husqvarna and went back to my old elementary school to extract remembered shapes from the floors of my youth. You might not have thought Deepak would instruct something like that, but you obviously wouldn't be the kind of Deepak scholar that I was, the kind unpolluted from mistaking his message by actually listening to and/or reading a single thing he ever said.

I remained pure to stay close to the truth.

I also carved up those floors good with that chainsaw. The bits that looked like the outline of a 78 Vega? I gutted those and put them on the outside of my rusted Citation to give it class. The weird varnish mark resembling a cowboy-era revolver? That I removed to make a casing for my Babolat tennis ball cannon, the one I always took to Laguna Beach on Father's Day. I gave in to all my impulses, so many years old, and took it all.

Of course, that didn't leave the current student children much to stand on. What could I do though? Thinking of them would have meant failing to actualize myself. What sense would that have made?

Kids today are so coddled already.

Frog Legs are Good Though It's Hard to Get a Grip to Bite if They Aren't Dead First

Let me state right from the start that the Eiffel Tower does not have any signs prohibiting gerbil enthusiasts from bungee jumping off the second-tier deck via a cord made from used Olympic decathlon athlete underwear elastic. The signs all say no throwing objects, as that can be fatal to all the private detectives dressed in giant chipmunk costumes scurrying on the ground below to frighten Spanish tourists, but bungee jumping is jumping not throwing.

Don't even get started on subtext. Prohibition signs should not utilize subtext. Al Capone taught me that back when he subbed for Mrs. Keebler in third-grade microwave cooking class.

I mean, it isn't as if the tower isn't all bent up anyway, even before using it as a bungee cord mount. The sides didn't used to slope like that. Ever since they let John Waters film *Saucy Godzilla Versus the Cosine of a Sodomite Right Triangle* there, the girders have been a bit stressed.

Personally, I think throwing me in a Turkish malachite polisher prison was downright unjustified. You can tell me that's all specified in subsection seventy-three, eighty-two six bis of the Napoleonic bro code, but we both know that "bis" is an imaginary number anyway. I won't be fooled by Algebra again, not after that run-in with those bat-plastic-pants salesmen. I never should have trusted anyone smoking a cigar, let alone three of them.

Should an arresting officer even be wearing pink hot pants with plaid? Shouldn't they at least be his own, or at least cover his multiple sets of genitals? You're suspect, Frenchy.

I told all that to Inspector Clouseau, making sure to also submit each of my points written in triplicate on the back of a

Starbucks breakfast menu card, but I don't think he listened. Maybe that's because he was only on *The Pink Panther Show* playing on some English kid's laptop as the real French sandwich and chocolate truffle smorgasbord police drug me by.

It's kind of hard to say.

All I know for sure is that I won't be patronizing that tower in future with my hard-earned Susan B. Anthony commemorative two-dollar coins. Part of that is the muscle-bound cherubim with the flaming sword they posted at the entrance to keep me out, but part is also the fact that they only accept Euros.

I don't usually carry play money.

Sidney Poitier Wanted to See *Das Schwein* When We Went to the Movies Last Month, But That Was a No-Go Since I Just Made That Title Up Right Now

I went to unwrap the Christmas ham this year, but the plastic wrapper just kept going. I thought the packaging had gotten perhaps a bit overfed, but then I reached the middle and didn't find any meat. No ham at all. It was only cellophane and packing tape the whole way in, rolled in layers like Pharaoh Ramses II. That certainly wasn't what I'd paid for.

So I took it back to the store. The Sears and Remington Roebuck Yarn Supply Outlet I'd visited wasn't open anymore, so I broke into the Harbor Tool, Unrefined Sugar, and Freight next door instead. They were closing up shop too, but George Hamilton was still un-stacking the chairs from atop the tables where he'd put them to mop. Surprised him a bit when I broke in the still open doors.

Oddly enough, he was actually the one who'd sold me the ham in the first place. Guess he moonlighted a bit on his days off.

I put George in a quick headlock when he tried to run. Flight was a clue something was really amiss rather than a simple mistake having occurred. People forgot to put hams in wrappers all the time and it wouldn't have been a big deal, simply issue a replacement through the mail and give me some free leg-waxing coupons. Colonel Sanders ran into the situation at least once a month and he did fine. It was certainly nothing to flee the country to Bora Bora and open a light-less tanning bed empire over, not for something so (hopefully) easily fixed. I found plane tickets and a hundred dollar's-worth of French francs in one of George's pants pockets though, the twenty-pound ham in the other.

Busted.

Turned out, George didn't have a license to sell hams over fifteen pounds. He wouldn't get that without another ten credit hours in criminal justice at the night school/chewing gum recycling station downtown. He needed the extra money from large ham sales over the holidays though for that cosmetic blood transfusion he'd been hoping for, so he sold anyway… just with no ham so he didn't get in the really big trouble.

He was more afraid of the Livestock and Agriculture Advisory Board than of the white-collar fraud squad.

Regardless, I simply beat him up with a VHS box set of the original unaired episodes of *The A-Team* and took the ham, so it all came out okay. The LAAB couldn't call that a sale, now could they? That way even George had to be happy with it.

Billy Bush taught me that trick.

X-Ray Machines Stay Crunchy, Even in Commuter Lanes

You ate your morning cereal out of a pothole in the middle of Colfax Street because all your Tupperware was dirty and Carlos Mencia filled your dishwasher with rubber cement again. Just walked right out there into traffic and filled it full of Cap'n Crunch and two percent milk, cereal first because it only floats on top otherwise. Then you chowed down like Indira Gandhi that time she tried Applebee's, using a titanium replica of a massive Pacific geoduck shell as a spoon.

You found the meal tasty, extra crunchy from the loose bits of asphalt and the NSA encrypted flash drives someone had dropped in there, but you became concerned about the effects of all that corn syrup on the structural integrity of the pavement. You did, after all, swear endless vengeance when you were seven against Muammar Gaddafi and the cavity creeps for what they did to Twiggy. That's when you committed your life to becoming a street dentist.

Mind you, you didn't mean a roving dentist like Richard Branson who grabs random people walking in Central Park and performs orthodontic work on the fly using polyurethane and vintage Erector Sets. No, street dentist as in a dental professional for the street itself…more like Julia Grant.

Anyway, you went right to it. You looked for bits of decay with your official former president Taft jeweler's loupe, scraped it away with the shell replica you'd been eating with and using to cause all the trouble in the first place, and topped it all over using Gorilla Glue and the fanciest of large grain oatmeal. The American Dental Association will probably have your ass for that, but you've never been afraid of them… certainly not after the positions they took at their 978th annual convention on your pet crocodile and flossing during meals.

The traffic you simply waved around, needing the room to work, telling them that you were trying to rescue a microscopic civilization of baby ducks who all looked like Jerry Lewis but sounded like Patrick Swayze huffing argon. They were pretty good about it, which is understandable given that you were basically naked.

You never get dressed until after breakfast.

And all this is fine, but you wonder why I'm pointing it out. There's no reason really. I'm simply making conversation here in the street while I wait for the "Don't Rhumba While Wearing Vinyl Leisure Suits" light to change.

You okay with that?

Sacramento Jails Will Always Organize Kombucha Parties Absent Lumbago

Everyone loves white elephant parties, but few people stop to think about the cost the white elephants themselves have to pay for such things. We in the modern era do not have the luxury that our forbearers did of thinking the white elephant was a non-sentient being. Yul Brynner proved conclusively otherwise in his Skinner box experiments during the latter half of the Ford administration. Now we have to either change how we act, or admit that we simply don't care.

First off, think how caustic all that bleach is for the elephants. They're all born gray, and you don't want to know what it takes to change them. You can say that the elephants want to be pretty all you like, but they don't. They're only conforming to the unrealistic beauty standards put forth by the false media these parties are validating, the ones that Photoshop real elephant models and perpetuate despicable elephant color dysmorphia. Besides, that bleach could better be used for Tom Selleck's laundry.

And we can't forget the drugs and promiscuity. It may seem cute to get these elephants all hopped up on Pudding Roll-Ups (pudding in disguise) and watch them make sweet love for our viewing amusement, but it destroys lives. So many promising elephant scientists have lost their careers that way, many more than from paper grocery bag recycling initiatives. Elephant rehab is expensive too. Do you know how big a building you need for that? The real estate costs alone require a fortune, and we won't even count the price of elephant therapists.

Beba Ezzedin has been gone a long time anyway.

And it's all to keep us entertained anyway. What's *holiday* about it? What's *festive*? It's just like those old *Popeye* cartoons where he washes up on a South Seas island and uses his tomato soup fortune to pay the indigenous population to hide their limbs in landscaping planters. That's European colonialism at its most unapologetic, my friends. Don't tell yourself any different.

Of course, I have to go to one myself this afternoon. I wasn't going to, but I accidentally ate the RSVP form before I could click "no." That's what I get for skipping lunch. Now I have to engage in atrocities myself.

I wouldn't want to be rude.

The Las Vegas Strip Disappeared This Morning

The Las Vegas Strip disappeared this morning, leaving a large number of pasty white vacationing Midwesterners blinking bleary-eyed confused at the morning sun. It happened suddenly, monolithic towering casinos and flashy digital nickel slots evaporating like people's money normally did there. No lights, no bells, no "thwacking" of stripper cards advertising dancers that would come to your room but depicting women who were young in the early eighties.

No "you bring the booze, we bring the girls."

Apparently, that Joshua tree out on Interstate 15 that dreamed the whole town took a break for the first time since that Honeymooners debacle back in the fifties. Pulled up root and got itself a room at a motor lodge and pinewood derby car museum near Baker, closed all the blinds and watched countless hours of HBO original programming. Without its dreams, Vegas was nothing more than a single-story collection of housing developments, gas stations, and *Speed Racer* themed massage parlors.

And a mass of bewildered tourists wandering around in the empty desert like Lawrence of Arabia that time he lost his GPS unit.

Fremont street was still there, of course. Binions and Golden Gate. Four Queens. That place was too ugly to be a dream, too greasy to disappear. It lingered, like herpes or DVD collections of *Alf*.

The casino conglomerates ran to the mayor. The mayor ran to the mob, which was a short trip. The mob sent Dean Martin and Robert DeNiro to knock on the Joshua tree's motor lodge room door with 1967 World Series commemorative softball bats, break a few kneecaps if they had to. Joshua trees didn't have kneecaps, but Martin and DeNiro managed to be convincing anyway.

It would have been a terrible thing if the rains never came again, or if someone were to release the Joshua tree's credit card information online.

Regardless, the Joshua tree went back to its place on Interstate 15 and resumed dreaming. Put down desert roots again. Raised a family of adopted Belgian refugee children.

And the dream of Las Vegas bloomed from nothing again, like the resurgence of bell-bottoms. Neon and two hundred foot tall cement. Cocktail waitresses dressed like reflective genies. Cocaine and thalidomide in the bathrooms. A Cirque du Soleil version of the Gettysburg address with an all bonobo monkey cast. The tourists went back inside.

And they spent money. Sometimes their own.

Luck was a lady again, an eighty-year-old lady wearing a gold lame track suit covered in Faberge rhinestones and an LED tiara seventy feet tall filled with the blood of male atheist virgins. All was right and well once more.

David Duchovny Borrowed my Micro Machines and Never Returned Them

Denver's first snow was only supposed to be a half-inch in the city, but that half-inch ended up being more like ten feet. Lucky I had that Hot Wheels track set from the late seventies out in the garage. Otherwise, I might have starved to death when I couldn't get out of my townhome.

The rest of my food was all gone after entertaining that shampoo and mirrored dress shoe trade delegation from American Samoa. The event went well, but I think it was really a catfish so they could see me in my Fruit of the Looms. We'll see if I end up actually being their sole distributor in the restroom of the Joliet Stuckey's, but they ate a lot in any event.

They left my cupboards bare and ate all my food too.

That Hot Wheels track set sure came in handy then. People forget those things were made of old spaghetti noodles with just enough xanthan gum thrown in to make them flex a bit and some OJ to color them orange. You have to boil them a while to soften the tracks up, but it works eventually. The red connector pieces too, high-grade thin plate beef jerky.

This is only true of the late seventies sets, of course. They switched to polyurethane somewhere around '79 after that diabetic kid went into a coma. He hadn't eaten his tracks or anything, but the company wanted to show moral support. You know how it was, what with all those people falling in the Cola Wars. It was a hell of a time, but the edible Hot Wheels track sets had to go in the interests of national morale.

I guess I came out good years before at the Armani armpit swap meet and incontinent albino roller derby celebrity invitational in Puyallup. What would I had done if the set had been from 1982?

A lesser person might not have starved being trapped for only a day until the local V.F.W. samurai brigade came to dig the city out, but I've got a blood sugar thing these days. I crash hard if I don't eat every 75 minutes, and tend to do something drastic like gnaw off my own foot two or three times. No, it was a good thing I had a backup plan in the garage.

Besides, I was able to entertain myself running a few cars down the tracks while they were sticking out of the pot, softening enough that they'd slide all the way down inside. That was nice, even if the boiling water took the paint off a few of the cars.

Damn cheap lead pigments.

Still, could have been worse. Right?

The Electoral College Has Nothing to Do with Regulating Water Recreation on Lakes No Matter What the Ski-Doo Company Would Have You Believe

"Finally! Now look, you guys sold me that 150 In One Electronic Project Kit and you've got to do something about it. I've been on the phone two hours already and those sheep have almost chewed their way through my pantry door. If you don't send Dana Carvey soon, I'm toast."

"What? Yes, I realize you don't actually have stores and thus weren't technically the people who *sold* it to me. That was Thurgood Marshall in the alley behind the St-Hubert in uptown Ottowa, had it hidden under his judicial robes…and nothing else. However, it's still your product, so what does that matter?"

"Yes! I followed the directions to the letter! Even the ones in cuneiform! I wrapped each tungsten wire around the correct nuclear-contact post, inserted the appropriately-banded marsupial resistor, recited Lord Nelson's prayer backward, cut the head off a Tanzanian blood cabbage, and cast the "charm self" spell. That's when the anti-matter wormhole to Eugene, Oregon opened and the demonic chlorophyll hybrid conservative party attack sheep started pouring out *and* not a single one of the experiments worked. Right, not the siren, the crystal radio, or even the binary adder. Not a one."

"Of course, I checked that I hadn't plugged it in backward! That's the *first* thing I tried! Do you think I'm Fritz Lieber or something?"

"No…you're right, I'm sorry. I realize that your job is very difficult, what with having to keep the Huns out of the breakroom and Jerry Lewis always trying to steal your wallet. I understand, I do. I empathize. It's just that those sheep make me nervous."

"I'm allergic to bite wounds."

"What? Sure, I suppose I could try putting it all back together again from scratch after rubbing the parts with electrified tin foil. Hang up and call back afterward? All right, if that's what the procedure is. I hope I can beat the sheep. Do I call you back direct?"

"Certainly, I'll hang on for that survey once you disconnect."

If the Prefix of Prostate Implies it's Prosthetic, Then Why Do I Keep Waking Up With My Giant Pancake Gone?

I broke down due to hunger and tried one of those hard candies from the bulk section of Albertsons the other day, but it didn't really have any flavor. Wasn't even sweet. Looking closer at it, after I took it back out of my mouth, of course, I discovered it was a glass statue of a tiny otter. All the bins were full of glass animals of various colors and varieties. The otter had no sharp edges or anything, so I wasn't cut, but I have to say I was a bit concerned.

Lucky I don't bite after that kid sued me back when I was passing myself off as a postgraduate owl.

There was a clerk nearby that I notified while he was busy constructing a diorama of the significant battles of the Peloponnesian War out of old Schlitz beer cans, but he said they were aware of it and working on the problem. I demanded to know what he was talking about since either you removed glass animals and replaced hard candy or didn't, not really being a progressive solution kind of situation, and that's when I noticed he was Scott Bakula.

Scott begged me not to tell anyone once he realized I saw through his "not Scott Bakula" sticker disguise. Apparently, he hadn't been able to get any new acting gigs since he did that risqué comedy about Pope Clement V's baccarat hobby and he had run completely out of cash. He had to sell his mansion in that Cincinnati junkyard and therefore had nowhere to store his glass animals. They were valuable, he insisted, each naturally formed from a unique process by which Edmund Muskie's skin-secreted toxins. Since Ed was dead now, there would never be any more than what Scott had.

Irreplaceable, and in high demand due to Obama's nutmeg tariffs.

But Scott didn't want to be forced to sell, not like what he had to do with his third nipple when the Pendleton don called his Buffalo Bills Super Bowl bet in around Easter. The bulk hard candy aisle seemed like a certain savior, what with the country swearing off all sweets since Wilford Brimley hired that mad potato scientist from Latvia to give everyone diabetes.

Who would know?

Too bad Scott wasn't aware that careful diet management and cybernetic bowel replacement surgery allowed a person to splurge once in a while, leading me to discover his little scheme. He wouldn't though; he's only Scott Bakula.

It's not as if he's Bill Bixby or anything.

We Should Have Known What Would Happen When Schrödinger Said He Was Writing a Book About the Brontosaurus

Driving past all the center-pivot irrigation rigs in central Nebraska, I kept imagining what it must have looked like all those years ago when those gentle giants roamed the Earth. Modernly there were only their bones where those poor creatures came to rest when they reached their sell-by dates, but once those bones were once covered in skin and teeth and Lorna Doone shortbread cookies. They might not have been the savage meat-eaters that the Kansas/Oklahoma oil pumpjacks were, but their sheer size alone must have truly been a thing to behold.

I've read that center-pivot irrigation rigs were able to get as big as eight acres in length and would roam as far as a hundred square miles in search of the silver alfalfa beans they most preferred.

Of course, I didn't have an advanced degree in large-scale industrial equipment paleontology. It was more of a hobby, like Harold L. Ickes and tennis doubles partners least-square maintenance minimum tree-spanning algorithms. I'd done my research though, and I always stopped to admire the rigs.

But then, who didn't?

I found it amazing that each was born with a specific date when their lives would cease like that, sell-by dates to prevent spoilage before a customer could get them home. I wished we could have implemented something like that for yogurt or other dairy products, even raw chicken feet, but I knew how resistant Telly Savalas would be to such a thing. He always railed against big radio-frequency government, and he did have a point. Also, surely that aspect of those creatures, at least as much as the buildup of leftover doughnuts in the world's anthracite volcanoes, led to the end of the Hydrogenated Age.

After all, where would humans be if that was still going?

Those immense beasties created the plains by flattening the Pliocene uric acid mountains left by the carbolic soda floods with their tremendous bulk. Could we have survived alongside them without being squished? We'd have been as crushed as Steve Guttenberg's long-haul trucking career. It was best not to even think what those sell-by dates implied about the concept of intelligent design, but they certainly did those of us at the Vatican Kevlar G-string crochet league a few favors.

It was the best thing for us since the Huguenots outlawed the Krebs cycle.

Christine Nöstlinger Got In Trouble With the EPA Once They Found Out Conrads Had Been Leaking Into the Soil and Water Supply For Years

Go ahead and be jealous. I've got me one of those five-year-old Barack Obamas that are so big this year. I had to camp out in front of Blockbusters for a week straight to get one. That's why they're so hard to find, both limited supply and no one knows where there's a Blockbusters anymore.

Cutest five-year-old "president" ever.

I can't believe it took them this long to come out with these. I mean, what else would you use cloning for? Sheep? Organ replacement? Five-year-old clones of one of the coolest presidents of the modern era is a no-brainer, even if they all do come with that disclaimer than no political power is included and the clones are for entertainment purposes only.

We all love it when he talks about wanting to be president someday. The little tyke just doesn't know he already was, sort of. It's cute, but it's also kind of sad, his glory days actually being completely behind him. I always take mine out for ice cream every time it happens. Then again…maybe the little bastard does know and has simply been playing me the whole time.

Never trust a clone. Thanks, Obama.

The biggest problem is emptying out the gun storage room in the basement when it gets full. He may not really be president, but the neighbors' guns still somehow keep ending up down there anyway. He denies knowing anything about it, but I'm still suspicious.

It feels downright dangerous at times. I never know when

one could go off.

Still, it's all worth it in the end because he's so darn adorable. Who could say no to that face? Who? Well, probably the five-year-old John McCain clone I also bought…but I keep those two separated.

That's just good parenting.

This Story Keeps Using the Name of "Achilles, Agony, and Ecstasy in Eight Parts" as Its Title No Matter How Much I Take Away Its Coachella Privileges

I'm really not sure what I should do at this point, short of going to court to have this story ruled ungovernable and sent to juvenile cake-decorator's prison with Paul Newman and that guy I keep confusing with the Skipper. I mean, no matter how much I beat it with fluorescent lamp cords, ground it to Wrigley Field, yell Finnish obscenities, convert its 401K diversification to entirely Inacom Corporation stock, or anything else reasonable, it still keeps using the name of that damn Manowar song as its title.

Of course, keep in mind what Lewis Carroll and seven of the current sitting Supreme Court justices would say about the name of a song versus its title, what either or the song itself is called, and the best way to get from Lincoln to David City by hovercraft.

The story is only being willful. It knows that it lost the right to select its own title in that cerulean-rules poker game. I'm not the one who made the bet. Though, why it agreed to a game where I bludgeoned it with a fifteenth-century Damascus iron fire poker until it submitted was a mystery to me…much like this story's obsession with that ridiculous song title.

After all, the song isn't bad, but it's not "Copacabana" or anything. We all know Manowar wanted to call it "The Poky Little Puppy and How It Grew," falling back on the actual title when the twenty-seven lawyer team combining the full amalgamated political power of Janette Sebring Lowrey and Margaret Sidney burned down their outhouse annex while they were at that tulip festival scouting out the northwest passage through downtown traffic during rush hour.

So why is this story so big on it? No one else is, particularly Hector.

But here we are regardless, the story still holding out to get its spoiled-brat way. If things don't change soon, I think I'll call one of those famous English nannies. I hear they kill for as little as a used 87 Volkswagen and a pot of clotted cream.

Eugene Belford Would Consider it a Personal Favor if You Didn't Believe This True Story Because it Stole His Lunch Money and Called Him an Incorporated Bandicoot Bedsore

Barbara Streisand broke an empty Stroh's bottle over my head one Saturday in 1972. We were in a neighborhood dive bar on 50th and Center watching the Buffalo Bills win the 1975 World Series of Poker and ended up disagreeing on whose turn it was to eat the CORN NUTS. Apparently, it turned out to be Barbara's, though only because I decided to be the bigger person once the head wound took hold. It's totally true, even if no one would believe it due to that federal injunction.

Wait, I might be thinking of Robert Blake.

It's just like that time Josephine Baker and I were playing Nerf joust on the Galaxy Orbit at Peony Park. She was cheating, running her coaster car backward unpredictably so she could catch me unaware. If I hadn't had Niels Bohr to rework the laws of physics for me, I would have lost for sure. Of course, then I went and blew my lead by falling off the top lighting rail over by the cotton candy concession.

Lucky Queen Isabella I of Castille was there to catch me… or am I thinking of Studs Terkel? It gets so hard to remember, what with the impact that *The Real World* franchise had on the Nikkei Index.

Anyway, so there I was…locked into a generations-long blood feud with Mahatma Gandhi and the Earl of Sandwich. Nikola Tesla tried to get a Pepsi out of the machine and accidentally sent us back in time to the 1898 Trans-Mississippi/ Siberian and International Glad Bag Exposition where we all ended up buying the same color Corvette sedan over by where you rode the swan boats. Obviously, we couldn't show up to the party in the same car, so we had to hunt each other down through the streets of a Pennsylvanian ghost town sitting atop an endlessly burning coal mine fire, popping occasionally out of abandoned wooden saloons to take pot shots at each other with vintage Pog dispensers. Then our attentions wandered and we all moved to the Grand Cayman Islands to open the world's first dairy bank and liquid-y cheese credit union, specializing in sheep milk related products.

But I got hungry, and that story is completely true. No one will believe it though, not after what Ivan Boesky did with that comet. I never should have agreed to film that Nebraska Public Access Television commercial…but I needed the money.

Bozo the Clown was going to do a live show at Octoberfest and them tickets weren't cheap.

Gummy Candies May be the Fourth State of Matter, But That's Only After They've Been Admitted to the Union

Due to my repeated ding-dong-ditch offenses harassing Nelson Mandela for his unquestioned support of predatory parrot apartment co-ops in the South Bronx, the International Monetary and Cotton Candy Fun and Part-Time Criminal Silicon Wafer Court sentenced me to life as a Hanna-Barbera cartoon. As part of a last-minute plea deal, they agreed not to actually animate me. Still, I was forced to organize my life according to the three-fold Hanna-Barbera principles.

I never should have picked Joe Piscopo as my attorney, especially given the size of his jelly bean retainer.

To begin with, I had to restrict myself to only the most basic bodily motions. Everything at the joints, torso held steady. When I ran, it had to be past the same place at least five times before going anywhere. The practice had me pretty close to following the Atkins Diet, but I did get to keep my second spleen.

I also had to pick a gimmick scenario and conform each day of my life thereafter to that pattern. Mine ended up being a life as a retired veterinarian where my pets were bumbling jokester secret agents for the bovine growth hormone and leave room for the holy ghost slam dance lobby. It was primarily a Bosley-type role, so fairly hands-off and low time commitment, but I did have to handle the occasional hijinks aftermath…like hiding the exsanguinated body of Grover Cleveland.

All in all, not the worst deal I could have gotten.

The hardest part was having credits roll each night before bed, accompanied by that jerky theme song played by The

Monkees. Do you know how hard it is to sleep through something like that? I sure do. Ended up developing a pain killer and off-brand cold medicine addiction just to knock myself out each night until it was over, which did not bode well for my campaign to be elected the next Republican Colonel Sanders.

And I do love that chicken so.

But, I only have myself and Nelson Mandela to blame. Mostly I save time and blame it all on Nelson. I mean, if he hadn't done what he did to those poor parrots, then I wouldn't have had to harass him in the first place.

Fair's fair.

You Can Digitize the Heroes of My Childhood Past But That Still Won't Get You Christmas Coupons for Free McDonald's Cheeseburgers Because the Age of Aquarius is Over, Man

Teddy Ruxpin set up a viral waffle laboratory in my garage to fight the Elf on a Shelf menace, but I just couldn't stop getting drunk and setting him afire.

Tremors Was Originally Supposed to be a Romantic Documentary, But Kevin Bacon Hates Citing Sources So They Just Said It Was Fiction

As much as I wanted to get back to Vietnam again, the decision to hold this year's corporate board meeting and AM/FM radio swap meet in the tunnels of Củ Chi seemed ill-advised. For one thing, there was barely room for us, and certainly not the presentation slides. Frank talked in the dark while Sammy, Joey, Dean, Peter, and I crawled behind. That was the other thing, Frank was Frank Sinatra.

I think you can put together the full names of the rest of the Rat Pack.

Several times I initiated a motion to remind Frank that "Chairman of the Board" was an honorific nickname only and that there was no actual company to lead, no profits to report upon, no reason to hold annual board meetings. As usual, though, the motion was tabled for a later date in favor of yet another martini lunch. None of these guys wanted to face facts. I think they all dreamed of being a used car salesman as kids and only had to drop out of community college accounting courses to become crooners when their mothers needed new press-on-nails transplants.

And also, as usual, Frank had Dean give me a wedgie when I brought up the concept. It'd become such a traditional part of meetings that I didn't even mind anymore. It ceased hurting once I had my buns sewed together on shore leave in Maui.

I showed them.

Another motion I continued presenting without any hope

of getting addressed was why the hell they made me come to the meetings. I was never in their group, not even having been born until the seventies whereas most of their group were actually dead already. It was nonsensical. But, Frank just told me, as usual, to go ahead and make a note about it in the minutes. I know that's only for show though.

After all, they took minutes on a cold bowl of sauce-less spaghetti, and Dean was eating it at the time.

The whole situation was hopeless. If it wasn't for the frequent flyer miles, I wouldn't have even gone anymore. After another two or three more board meetings, I'd get a free flight to Des Moines on an alternate Saturday of my choice having a full moon falling between November fourth and January second, middle seats only, at two a.m. Chinese Standard Time (blackout periods possibly applicable).

Then all I'd need would be a reason to take that flight.

The Quickest Way to a Man's Heart is to Turn Left at Pecos and Follow the Roundabout

What made me a monster? Was it all those hours of *Turbo Teen* and the *USA Cartoon Express*? My parents feeding me Kix cereal instead of something decent couldn't have helped. Perhaps the sales tax policies of the late Carter administration? What made me so cruel, to take so much delight in the sufferings of others? It's enough to make me question my fitness for membership in the Columbia Record and Tape Club, no matter how much they welcome me.

I simply can't help myself, despite shoving handful after handful of Flintstones Chewables under my armpits. Home hydrotherapy and Freudian Fourier transform hasn't helped either.

I'm still a beast in short pants and a reflective fedora.

I don't even remember taking that story I'd written earlier that month, snatching him into some ancient Ford Econoline van with a painting of a wizard on the side. Sounds were suddenly coming from my basement while I was watching *Pitch Perfect* and I found it down there wrapped up against my furnace with scotch tape, its pants nowhere to be found. I was supposed to be revising it, but something else must have happened, something of which I had no recollection. I guess huffing fumes of dried out Coca-Cola from a Pioneer herbicide bottle will do that to a guy, regardless of any tolerance that's been built up.

But...why didn't I then let it go? Pull off the tape? It wouldn't have told anyone, its tongue missing from its mouth at that point anyway. If I released it, that story would have counted its lucky stars to simply be alive and fled, denying anything had ever happened like the Nixon staffers post 1974. If it was the drugs, then why did I keep going? Why did I go upstairs to fetch my Mr. T cheese tray and ornamental soapstone-carving tool set?

That thing was *supposed* to be for making my own Smurf figurines.

Instead, I used it to tear through that story's flesh, taking out word after word and showing them to it while it still lived. I must have cut its word count by half, but amazingly it was still breathing. Anatomy has always confused me.

I wasn't content with simply gutting it either. I mutilated its face with Ring Pops and the hydrochloric acid I normally used in baking brownies, giving it an entirely new title in the process. Maybe I wouldn't have gone that far if it hadn't kept spouting those *Austin Powers* quotes.

Regardless, why did I do it? I simply don't know. I can only hope that drawing that turtle on the matchbook to get me into that graphic design school at the Metropolitan Museum of Art fixes me. Otherwise, I'll have to end up taking that job at Monsanto after all.

The Concept of a Baker's Dozen is Elitist Since You Know They Only Took That Job Because They Couldn't Count Well Enough To Be the Attendant at the Tollbooth

The price of eggs rose a bit once that guy who played the lead in the *Starman* TV show figured out you could replicate an entire 80s sitcom inside a free-range hen's egg. It was quite a process, but not overly difficult. That made solitary eggs somewhat more valuable than an omelet though.

The discovery came about as a hobbyist attempt to make one of those Hanoi coffees, I believe.

Anyway, the first thing to do was make a hole at one end of the shell with a tinker's awl. Anybody else's awl would likely work as well, but the tinker owed a lot of favors and would likely loan his out. Next, the white had to be sucked out while leaving the yolk, just like at the Dundee elementary school annual track and field competition long jump event. After that, the show's theme song simply had to be whispered in through the hole.

I think it was Eddie Furlong who first found out egg yolks conformed to 80s sitcoms when their theme songs were sung. He didn't figure out the whole egg effect though, which was excusable since he was busy being Eddie. One needed the hole to let the song in and let out the white, which had to go in order to make room for the song to be able to contact the yolk.

It seems so simple now, but I find it important to repeat that Eddie never figured it out.

Personally, I started with *Good Times* first. That was not

80s though, so I had to give up and try something else. I still have the bruises. *Perfect Strangers* was my next attempt, and the characters' egos fit well inside an egg, so Don Johnson and I were good to go.

Admittedly, it was hard to decide on a shared visitation schedule that kept the two of us happy.

Still, it did screw with the world egg market rates for a while. Lucky only free-range ones worked. Otherwise, we'd have all turned isotropic cannibal pretty fast.

A show's a show, but we all gotta eat.

Powerball Got More Interesting When Co-Winners Had to Battle to the Death Highlander-Style Rather Than Share

Rosie Perez tried to warn me about the Publishers Clearing House sweepstakes, hid secret messages made of red velvet cake batter and old Vaseline between frames of *White Men Can't Jump*. That was about how unlikely it was to win though. Rosie didn't say jack for the other possibility.

Lulled into complacency, I thought nothing of going to work instead of quitting my job and everything else in life to wait 24/7 for the prize van. Who wouldn't, right? Well, not only did they not leave the check when they dropped by to find me away, they broke in and stole all my shit.

That's right, apparently burglary finances all the prizes they hand out. If the Publishers Clearing House prize van finds an unguarded house on the route of winners, they take rather than give. They even burn the house to the ground and salt the earth so no crops will ever again grow.

They don't fool around.

Supposedly it was all spelled out in the entry materials, hidden under a stamp for a round-the-world zeppelin jousting trip on page seventy-three, near some of the optional bill-me-later *TV Guide* magazine subscription checkboxes. Failure on my part to read didn't render them liable for their acts, or so their attorneys insisted as Ed McMahon tied me to a railroad trestle and flogged me with steel-coated Red Vines licorice ropes.

Oh yeah, Ed isn't really dead after all. He simply had to pretend he was until he learned to control the terrible rage within him. He's not doing so good at that yet and mentioned the trauma of having to laugh at Johnny Carson for so many years when I suggested he was confusing himself with *The Incredible Hulk*.

Anyway, that prize didn't work out so well and Rosie Perez was no help at all. I can only hope that the *Reader's Digest* sausage-frying botulism contest goes better when the drawing happens next week.

It's the only shot I've got.

It's Unwise to Form Land Treaties With Sugar Gliders Outside of An Attorney-Client Relationship as Their Tory Politics Entitle Them to Preferential Treatment in Admiralty Courts

The whole mess with the tiger flex spending account began at The End, that crappy dive bar over on Twenty-third Street. The mixed drinks were usually diluted with dihydrogen monoxide and benzene, but the peanuts were free and the drafts were only two dollars (two dollars!) so we went there frequently. There was usually something entertaining going on, like that night when Florence Henderson and Diego Rivera were street brawling over whether Charles Darwin or Alfred Russel Wallace was more influential to the evolution of soft rock in the eighties.

That's when Oliver Cromwell restored order by throwing us all in prison.

Granted, it wasn't bad as far as prisons go. We had rooms next to the beach and all our drinks and meals, other than the sushi bar, were included in the price of our stay. We just had to keep our wristbands on. Technically, it was more of an all-inclusive prison resort. Of course, it was located on a frozen rocky crag just slightly to the north of Greenland and a bunch of guys who all looked like Roger Moore beat us constantly using bent television aerials and leftover pasta, but still.

I'd been locked up in worse.

Luckily, one of the guys who looked like Roger Moore actually was Roger Moore. He was working undercover for the Mossad to free Wesley Snipes, who was conveniently incarcerated with us on a polychromatic jaywalking charge. The orders said nothing about us, but we walked out right along with them after Roger killed all the guards and blew a hole in the main wall using a 1968 Democratic National Convention commemorative crowd-dispensing Nerf ultimate Frisbee safety bug bomb and kitchen blender.

Fuck the dumb shit, right?

We all got back to the bar in time to see the end of the game, our drinks still cold, though we had to pay the bus driver extra Detroit Tigers gin rummy players since it was during peak hours, and that was the first place the authorities would and did look for us, so maybe it was a pretty stupid choice after all.

But, hindsight is always 20/20…just like fortified wine.

Preheating Ovens Seems Like a Lot of Wasted Effort When You Cook Everything Other Than Pizza Rolls With Thermite Fire Anyway

The DEA told me I might have made that story about the quark and neutron rabbit living under my sink too concentrated. Apparently, a hundred people had already died. Overdose, the story containing more parts per million liquid absurdity compared to monosodium glutamate-based soft drinks than the FDA allows lab rats for Sunday brunches absent notes from their parents. Officer Lardass suggested I dilute things down a little.

And, though I appreciated the extra cash in being able to stretch a story a little further, it was still a hassle. I mean, I wasn't the one OD-ing. I wasn't Roald Dahl or anything.

The process required working baking soda into the text. No baking powder, easy to mix up but it would give people brain bubbles and cause more strokes than the series finale of *Charles in Charge*. A suspension of one-part words, one-part blank page, and two parts baking soda would yield the rated strength the DEA recommended.

The DEA always offers such helpful advice for dealers mixing their product.

But you can't just rub baking soda in there the way you can with instruction manuals for home anti-gravitational metal lathes. For some reason, the verbs will all oxidize quickly and you end up with a soggy, rusty mess. The only way it works it to keep oxygen off the letters until after the filler is chemically bonded within the story, seal it off from the elements.

So, of course, I had to suspend the story in half-and-half

while I cut it. The milk fat encapsulates the baking soda and blocks out air until the covalent bonds become ionic. I learned that from Linus Torvalds, though he sent me the instructions in a paint bucket of random bits that I had to assemble and compile into a coherent recipe myself.

That guy is such a pain.

We'll have to wait and see if it all worked though. No one has died yet since the re-release, but it's still early. A lot could change by the time daylight saving time rolls around on the East Coast.

It always does.

I Used to Ride That Horse a Lot Until He Got Too Full of Nickels and They Had to Put Him Back Down in the Basement of the Alamo

My neighbor when I was seven owned a bar downtown, but I don't think that had anything to do with the zoo he put together in his backyard. He didn't charge admission, but my parents still told me to stay out of there when they weren't around. I don't know if that was because they thought it was dangerous alone, or if it was because Lance Armstrong was kidnapping people for his socialistic SlimFast direct mail marketing railroad pyramid scheme, but they grounded me to my room anytime they caught me over there.

I spent the majority of that year restricted to my room, pretty much all the time I wasn't selling fake cigars on the floor of the Imperial Senate.

In truth, it was an odd kind of zoo. My neighbor didn't really have any animals. There were a few garter snakes, but only the ones that happened to be in his backyard anyway. My neighbor had nothing intentional to do with that, no matter what Robert Stack said. The exhibits were actually all faked, constructed laboriously out of smashed-up bricks, old television parts, and chopped church pews. I didn't know why I couldn't get enough of the place.

The "rhino" seemed particularly neat to me. My neighbor wired it all up with recycled electricity on a special 220 line. The reason for that was vague, as he hadn't assembled the parts into something animatronic or anything like that. He just jammed tubes and knobs and dials into the bricks and wood wherever they'd stay and then coupled wires to whatever conducted. It wasn't even shaped like a rhino, resembling more a topographical map of McDonald's drive-through locations in San Diego circa 1973. That was his "rhino" though, and the U.S. Olympic recumbent bicycle team was on hand constantly to eject anyone opining differently.

Though, no one ever did.

In fact, all the exhibits were pretty much like that, simply electrified assemblages of junk with a few garter snakes roaming around aimlessly. It was possible that I kept going over to the parking lot for the nearby steel mill instead and that all had nothing to do with my bar-owning neighbor, but there's no way to tell for sure anymore.

It's been such a long time since then.

The Secret Was That Checkers Was Stuffed Full of Millions of Hundred Dollar Bills the Entire Time

My fellow Americans, it is with a heavy heart and a mystified noggin that I, Winston Zeddemore, must respectfully decline the honor of being your next president of these United States. Though I am deeply honored by this amazing and unprecedented write-in campaign performed exclusively on take-out menus at every other Stuckey's in the Deep South, I regret to inform you that I will be unable to serve. I offer you all the use of my blue '47 Chevy convertible instead.

Really, who could have seen this coming? Did you all just get done watching *Ghostbusters* again? Is this some kind of unnecessary and unwelcome backlash against the remake?

(Seriously, if you didn't want a Samuel Beckett version performed entirely by inanimate mid-century modern used oil filters, you didn't have to watch it. You could have done something productive with your time, like re-spackle your appendix with Chiclets or teach tone-deaf emperor penguins to hum "Amazing Grace." Honestly, go *do* something and let Aquaman marry who he wants.)

To begin stating my reasons, as I'm sure I'll be required to do, I simply feel that this responsibility is more than I want for myself. I'm a simple man with simple desires, only clamoring for a steady paycheck. Forming national policy is not my line, and I may have taken on a few conflicts at my last job when it comes to things like the Environmental Protection Agency.

(Hi, Walter. How's it hanging? Poker Thursday?)

Besides, have you all forgotten that I'm an imaginary character from a popular 80s movie? Technically that means I'm not eligible to be president. I know the same thing happened with Jimmy Carter and people looked the other way, though there still is some debate going there, but let's not even open that can of worms.

In short, no.

You all, though again I am really flattered, will just have to accept one of the actual candidates. (Lord knows there are enough of them.) Getting out of your mess isn't that easy. What did you think this was, the Chapultepec Peace Accords?

Honestly.

If I Wasn't Allowed to Use the Waffle Irons to Make My Own Hockey Masks Then Someone Should Have Said Something Sooner

I got me a job making them metal mesh tables for patio furniture sets. You know, the fancy ones. Want to know a trade secret? We make 'em out of old waffles.

Seriously! I wouldn't have believed it myself if I hadn't seen it done, hadn't had my own hands in the batter, so to speak. That's industry humor. You get that along with a dental plan and a copy of the employee handbook when you get hired.

The tables start out with old waffles leftover from Sunday brunches at Perkins. Each one someone didn't finish, we buy up. Buttered and syrup-ed already or not, doesn't matter. It's cheap that way, and ecological too. No waste. We stick them together with a bit of waffle glue until we have a base mass the size of a tabletop. That's where the molten steel fired in volcanoes that open evil-filled portals straight into the brimstone of hell come in.

Funny, it's odd how many people haven't heard of waffle glue. How else do people think broken waffles get fixed? Do they just toss them whenever there's the slightest problem rather than even attempt the most basic repair? It's right there at The Home Depot, between the late Victorian-themed pornographic skiing magazines and that style of rubber doorstops that look like someone's been chewing on them a bit. People tend to overlook it because it blends in with the coffee machine oil, but it's still present on the shelf. Waffle glue.

Anyway, the steel is what actually what makes up the substance of the tables. The waffles are more of a guide for it. You pour the hot liquid metal on there and the waffle meat sucks it up, at least until the heat burns that away. The bits on the ridges around the pockets cool, forming the familiar delicate strands that look like the world's most complicated full-contact tic-tac-toe board.

Of course, that's all before the particle accelerators and hazmat receptacles move into the picture. I can't talk about that part though. It's classified.

It doesn't matter too much in any event, a job's a job and you do what they tell you like any other. The proceeds all go toward the interplanetary war effort anyway, even if there's only the one planet, or at least that's what the stuff all over my paystub keeps telling me. Maybe someday they'll remember to put an amount payable on there as well so I can actually cash one.

It'd be nice.

The Title Was Pretty Misleading Since the Guns Used in Filming Were All About As Old as Most Commonly in Use and No One Took Their Boots Off At Dinner

I charged off into the woods to find the Smurfs when I was seven. My grip on reality was tenuous enough, and the actual existence of William Shatner was enough to push me over the edge. I was going to take moon pebbles to mark my way back, but my parents wanted me to take breadcrumbs from loaves baked during the French Revolution instead.

I began to suspect them at that point.

Not that it mattered anyway. The woods were only a block-thick strip of bushes with a couple pine trees running next to the steel mill, tattoo parlors, and high-level home blender emporiums. If you could get lost, it was because you didn't want to be found.

Like when Amelia Earhart faked her death to dodge student loan debt from ITT Tech.

Anyway, no Smurfs there either…though there was Charlie Sheen skulking about pretending to be one. He'd dyed his hair white and painted himself blue with poster paint, also got a bit of a beer belly and sniffed a lot. Said he was preparing for a role in the new *Smurfs* movie, but we both knew there'd be no movie with that Smurf-Berry Crunch cereal asbestosis litigation still pending. Said to call him Papa as well, which made me maintain a safe distance for entirely different reasons.

Winning being the least of them, tiger blood second.

Then Charlie laid out his blueprints for the village, all the exotic dancers and adult film stars who were going to move in. He plotted endlessly how to name them, but I thought the made-up names they already had were pretty smurfy as things stood.

Though, Flexxxy the Smurf probably wouldn't fly.

In the end, I turned his offer to join the town. For one thing, the cops were hovering nearby. For another, I'd rather play Gargamel like usual and figure out how to turn Charlie's corpse into gold.

All I needed to do was find someone to be Azrael.

Juan Valdez Used to Deliver Newspapers, But the Sandinistas Kept Complaining About the Way He Rolled the Sunday Coupon Inserts

The first time the Martians killed Ronald Reagan, I was on my beach vacation in Laramie. Wyoming didn't have any oceanfront of course, but that was the brilliance of my plan. Everyone knew it would become coastline property once all the Walmart checkers finally got a restroom break and the resulting flood drowned ninety percent of the Earth's population, so why not beat the rush? Prices were dirt cheap, though swimming was painful and Mr. T charged me a heck of a deposit on that Ski-Doo rental. I believe the Martians ate Reagan that time.

The second time the Martians killed Reagan, they did it with arterial lard blockages smuggled in through the G.I. Joe AM radio headsets he couldn't stop chewing on between takes filming *Degrassi Junior High.* Never knew why he hung out on the set so often when he wasn't even in that show, but I was busy in the Peace Corps in Sweden apologizing to all the starving orphans who'd been aggressively beaten in high-stakes Texas hold 'em poker games by Sally Struthers. She was such a sore winner and those kids had more than enough problems already. I just tried to do what I could, what any good person would have done, much like Reagan and that Radio Shack do-it-yourself cattle heart stint insertion kit.

At least it meant something the third time the Martians killed Ronald Reagan. They bartered engine improvements for the 1983 Honda Civic to Phyllis Schlafly in exchange for the right to do away with Reagan once again. Nancy was against the trade, but gas prices were soaring and the country needed help. What choice did Phyllis have? I took the bus at the time so I stayed out of the debate, but it was still a heavy burden for the local chapter of Rotary. Then again, most things involving Reagan were.

The next eighty-seven times the Martians killed Reagan felt excessive. The methods weren't even original, all simply comprising feeding him to their hamsters. They came up with different Martian-sounding names each time, like "Ma'atok," "Aaaruum," and "Gwen," but we all knew it was the same made-up bullshit ritual over and over. I personally thought they were just too cheap to buy real hamster food.

Honestly, I wish those Martians would go ahead and leave poor Ronald Reagan alone. Haven't they killed him enough? How much of the Martian's shenanigans should Reagan be expected to shoulder?

I think it's gone too far already.

Excursion Tours Don't Like It When You Put Quincy Down as Your Primary Physician

It was time to get my appendix taken out. I wasn't sick or anything, but all the kids were getting it done. Fashion. I simply wanted to be cool, just like when I had that third pineal gland implanted to be more like Henry Winkler.

My doctor was pretty competent, at least when he wasn't huffing ground-up circuits out of old ColecoVision units, but I still wanted to keep a close eye on him. Make sure he did the job right, you know? I wired myself up to a Yamaha Jet Ski battery and hooked his scalpel to a piezoelectric buzzer.

Like in the game, get it? Don't touch the sides? (Pervert.)

That's when I realized that there were no sides. My abdominal cavity didn't have an appendix-shaped hole over the top. Maybe I had some kind of harmless birth defect or something from my dad's Agent Orange habit, like Elijah McCoy. The doc was going to buzz the moment he touched me to start cutting, right or not. That poor guy was going to be so confused.

That would never do.

Then it came to me. I had Henry IV tattoo the appendix-shaped outline on my torso, in the right spot of course. No sense doing something like that halfway. It was cool, Henry owed me one since he broke my riding lawnmower last time he borrowed it. Lancastrians tend to do that.

Once I had my outline, I started injecting the tissue inside with liquefied Big League Chew. Got enough in there that the flesh became an insulator as opposed to a conductor, and would hold for a couple weeks since I sunk it good and deep. That method didn't cause as much xanthan gum poisoning as Chewels.

Thanks to *Mr. Wizard* for saving my bacon yet again. That

show taught me so much.

After that, I was ready to go. If the doc touched any wrong spot during my surgery, the whole OR would know it. That was almost as good as being able to monitor the procedure myself. No pressure now, Doc.

Funny that with all the work I put into my own health care, my medical bills were still so high. Life didn't always make sense.

My Bank Started Filling Their ATMs With Dye Packs After They Remembered Where the True Balance of Power in the Relationship Lie and Honestly Didn't Like Me Very Much Anyway

My complimentary sleep mask ate my eyeballs on the flight to Dallas the other day. It left my eyelids unharmed though, so I still classified that trip as only my second most painful travel experience. Having to ride on Frontier as Benoit Mandelbrot's carry-on luggage still took first place, and it probably always would.

That dude just packed so much stuff.

Personally, I resisted using those things on planes. I could never sleep anyway and it made it just that much harder to spot the osteopathic assassins from competing airlines sneaking up on me. Finally, I decided to see what Gwyneth Paltrow had been making all that fuss about, why everyone else listened to her about *having* to use them. Too bad I hadn't done that before they started handing out the eyeball-eating ones as the freebies.

The less hungry ones were extra.

Granted, the "Made by the Eyeball-Eating Politely Cannibalistic Swiss Enterprises" label should have been a warning. Too bad I didn't read after Laurence Fishburne made me star in that paper doll remake of *Deep Cover* in his place using that adhesion contract he printed on a can of pizza-flavored onion Pringles. Beforehand would have given me a fighting shot, afterward being completely impossible.

I no longer had eyeballs to use for reading, remember?

Though, it was actually a completely painless procedure. It just sucked them up like peeled grapes without using teeth or anything. The experience could have been worse, and at least I would never have to look Paul Reubens in the eye anymore as he gave me my annual hernia check.

Be thankful for the blessings you've got, right?

Well, at least that's what Paul says he's doing. I kind of have to take his word for it now, though I should have checked before. I'm no longer able to read through his medical credentials to verify his licensed status.

Here's hoping it would check out.

"Fish and Chips" Means You Gotta Eat Both, Motherfucker, Not Either-Or

Did you know that Americans have to go through an extra customs line at the Heathrow Airport? It's in a fish-and-chips kiosk near the food court, so it's kind of easy to miss. Better hope you don't, but I'd have never seen it myself if the attendant hadn't called me over while I was writing my credit card numbers on my shirt front like all smart travelers do.

I mean, what if you lose your cards abroad? You'd be stuck with no way to pay for anything, right? This way you can just hold up your shirt at a restaurant for the waiter to see, just like Neville Chamberlain.

Apparently, the kiosk was where they did a currency check — make sure you weren't carrying an odd amount. There's a law in England about Americans and even amounts dating back to a disagreement over a solitaire game played during the War of 1812. Common law is full of pitfalls like that, which is why the English no longer let troops have playing cards. It was either that or no longer have wars, but that would be much harder to accomplish due to all the copper cabling they'd already run under the streets.

Expensive to switch it all out at this point. Who'd pay for that?

My wallet was a tad bit unbalanced, but the attendant was nice enough to hide a few pounds to fix things. Saved me from filling out a lot of declaration forms, and from having to pay both of my kidneys in fines. He still had to rough me up a bit since people were looking and all, but I understood the guy still had to do his job. It served me right for carrying that much money on me anyway rather than give it all to the Scottish cash coolie the government sent to find me at the terminal gate who'd meet up with me later.

I'm slow to learn, I suppose.

Other Americans from my flight walked by without stopping, but the attendant said Interpol always gave them enough rope to hang themselves by, let them step outside before nabbing them so they couldn't say they intended to check in but just needed to convert their power to AC first. Get them dead to rights, like Fran Drescher. Can't prove you paid? Tower of London for you then, and no the admission ticket still isn't free when you're being incarcerated there.

Really, some people.

And that's when he took pictures of my genitals, to have a record that I'd been processed, and sent me on my way. To think I'd almost gone down the west corridor instead. That would have been a bit of bad luck.

The Subtle Literary Criticism of Harriet Beecher Stowe in Warrant's "Uncle Tom's Cabin" Eludes All but the Most Advanced Civil War Era Romex Scholars

The smell of hot machine oil and tanned kid leather overwhelmed me when I checked into my room for the bi-annual People Who Mispronounce "Belgian Hot Dogs" Assistant's convention in downtown Puyallup. That struck me as odd since I hadn't yet called for a paid Victorian chimneysweep companion and set up my Care Bears restraint and spinal realignment gear. The hotel said they knew nothing, so I started rummaging around…only to discover all three members of Bell Biv DeVoe running a gloveless finger factory inside my mattress.

You know, gloveless fingers. They're like fingerless gloves but reversed. Beethoven (either the famous composer, the Saint Bernard from that crappy movie, or both) invented them after he went crazy huffing fermented raisin box air. Instead of making a glove and cutting off the fingers so your hands can stay warm but you can still touch things, you make a glove and cut off the glove to leave totally useless leather finger covers that barely warm anything and get in the way of almost any activity.

Not much of a market, really.

That's why Bell Biv DeVoe said they set up shop inside my mattress, that and the box springs didn't have enough room. Real estate and labor cost overheads made it almost impossible to manufacture anything inside the United States anymore. At the same time, Bell Biv DeVoe could no longer cross the border due to fallout from that incident with the red latex party balloons and Lauren Bacall. Faced with diminishing album royalties and a limited skill set including only music and advanced hand-related leather craft, what else could they do?

Right, they did that. Then they set up the gloveless finger sweatshop (with only them as workers) inside my mattress when that didn't work.

They begged me not to call the manager. Apparently, he used to roadie for them back in the early nineties and they still owed him five bucks they couldn't pay from a time he ran for sandwiches during a show at the Nebraska state fair. They offered me all the gloveless fingers I could use in exchange for my silence, but I told them I was cool.

I'm no snitch.

It turned out to actually be kind of nice. The mattress was more supportive that way, and they sang "Poison" all night. I slept like a baby, which is more than I can say for Jerry with that Guns N' Roses fish and chips cart operating out of his nightstand.

Who could sleep next to that?

You'd Have to Walk a Hundred Thousand Generic-Nineties-Band Miles to Get the Nutrition in Just One Bowl of The Proclaimers' Breakfast Cereal

There were no real problems with my powder room toilet to complain of, but I decided to start tinkering with it anyway, just to see if I could optimize performance a bit. Frankly, I blame that copy of *Zen and the Art of Toilet Repair* my wife picked up on accident at the Blockbusters Video that appeared for only twenty seconds to true believers in the middle of Times Square on Administrative Professionals' Day 2015. Whatever though. Everyone needed a hobby.

I mean, the float arm worked fine and all — cut off water flow when the tank reached the appropriate level. But, wasn't the high-pressure jet nozzle on the fill tube a bit faster in driving the tank to full? Didn't the helium help move the float itself out of the way more quickly so liquid could take its place? Didn't greasing cause it to cut through the air like a hot pig through a well digger's coal butter?

That's all the stuff that Einstein recommends in his basic guide though. I didn't stop there, not if I wanted to be serious. My application for a The Home Depot home equity line credit card was simply the first step.

Thomas Crapper would have been jealous, in addition to long dead.

And at that point, how could I not race my modified toilet in that gas utility access alley over by the granola and peanut fuel oil co-op? All those middle-aged white guys irradiating titanium alloy ballcocks and polishing wax rings, everyone knew what they did back there. Bet for pink slips. Winners made a fortune, losers had nothing to go on.

Me? I don't want to brag…but it's not bragging to say that there were forty-seven toilets sitting in my living room. That was a solid fact, similar to Ed Asner's system for predicting Hungarian troop movement patterns hidden in sneeze-particle Brownian motion. I went in there and just looked at them sometimes, reflect on that image of true success.

The image of a living room full of other people's toilets, just like at Graceland.

The Chief Exports of *Body by Jake* are Bauxite and Leather Radios

I wanted big muscles when I was ten, so I answered the ad in the back of that *Norbert the Narc* comic book for the Charles Atlas fitness system. It turned out that Chuck relied on dramatic tension, threats by a sand-kicking bully behemoth who wanted to steal your girl in order to frighten your body into growth. That might have worked well for Woody Allen and Al Pacino, but both can tell you it's mainly just for show. The muscles aren't really strong, merely puffed up with air and silica foam like a startled cat, and that whole conflict-based fitness regiment was too stressful for me anyway.

I got out of chartered accountancy for a reason.

No, things were much better for me when I found that Repeater Device in my neighbor's trash can under a bunch of rotten orange peels and 347 VHS copies of *A League of Their Own*.

That thing was brilliant. It simply took each movement your body made and made it do it over a hundred times. Some kind of series of springs and nichrome resistance wires, I think, a lot like those chest exercisers from the fifties but with more layers and gear systems. It seemed like another fitness gimmick, akin to the ThighMaster or sit-ups, but it really did the job for me. I didn't even end up minding that putrid rind smell, which strangely made me think of Grandma.

You see, it's not making your muscles lift a heavy weight that makes them strong. Just once and rest won't do much, like differential calculus. Not everyone knows that. You have to do something over and over in a short period. You exhaust the muscle, forcing the body to send in a replacement, a high-grade ringer. The ringer is much bigger than the muscle you had before, and it has to stay in place if the old one is too worn out and confused to go back on. You trick it. The ringer never would have signed a contract for full-time duty on what you pay, not with his pro-ball skill set, but it's a bit too late to do anything about it once he's sent into the game. He's trapped, has no choice. A lot like Louie Anderson.

Next thing you know, you're ripped. Sure, the spring coils leave scar tracks on the surface of the skin, but it's no pain no gain in fitness. That's just the way it is, as Fred Savage knows only too well.

I was the most muscle-bound kid in fifth grade, even had the gym teacher running laps for me instead of the other way around.

Of course, I lost it all and totally went to seed at age eleven when the mainspring broke. The entire Repeater Device fell apart and I couldn't use it anymore after that. Couldn't get any interaction going. I still drank tennis balls and titanium brake shoe shavings out of my Jack LaLanne hydroponic juicer, but it wasn't the same. The ringer muscles got F. Lee Bailey to void their expired contract and I was back to normal size before NBC Sweeps Week was over. Couldn't buy a new Repeator Device either since the FDA banned them as potentially correlated to falling pork belly prices in Ecuador.

Still, it beat going to the spa. Who has time for that kind of thing?

Big Wheel Keeps on Turning, Little Wheel Abandoned Its Spouse and Children to Pursue Its Dreams of Becoming a Part-Time Mime in Spain

It wasn't Saturday when Barney Miller told me to the secret of immortality in exchange for that Hobbit cartoon on Betamax and a package of Ding Dongs, but it was sure Saturday soon enough. It had to be; it's been Saturday ever since…even on Super Tuesday. Frankly, I think things are better that way.

See, Barney said for me to sit on the Saturday square of my Pete Rose string bikini desk blotter calendar/oil filter rack and refuse to move. That way, it would always be Saturday and time would never advance. If time didn't move, then I couldn't age. Thus, immortality. You know, just like it's laid out in Heisenberg's Uncertainty Principle. It's all pretty basic.

Well, there's also that bit about sacrificing one of *The Partridge Family* to the dark lord Astaroth using a Hickory Farms cheese serving set, but I was already going to do that anyway.

Admittedly, I thought Barney was yanking my chain, but it's been several hundred years since I started and I'm still fresh as a daisy. I've even married Donald Trump three times I looked so young. Luckily, he forgot everything that happened when he woke up each morning, like in that Adam Sandler movie about the Battle of Trafalgar, so it was no harm no foul. Still, that was pretty good proof of my suspended state, even if the Yakuza put a price on my head in that ad in the back of the *Weekly Reader*.

Christopher Lambert could be a nuisance, but his handlers

usually kept him in check. He just couldn't accept that *Top Gun* was only a movie and kept trying to act it out whenever he got near me. I would have worried about it more, but it was Saturday and I couldn't get too worked up about anything on the weekend.

Immortality had other costs as well. My butt was going numb and that Partridge Family reunion tour was never going to happen at that point. I could only hope those two things weren't related, but I was pretty well bound to acceptance either way.

I mean, it's not as if Paula Abdul was going to return any of my calls regardless.

The Other Option Is Vinyl Linoleum, but Face Facts and Admit That's Gross and No One is Going to Use It if They Can Afford Anything Else

The modern love affair with hardwood floors and stone tile may be a bit pretentious, but at least we're committing fewer atrocities against that race of carpet giants we found in the basement. We're still flaying their skin off to finish rooms in some of our homes, but not in anywhere near the vast numbers we did in the eighties. Small improvements are still improvements, especially where carpet giant atrocities are concerned.

We have Pam Grier to thank for that if I'm not mistaken.

What? Didn't you know where carpet came from? Don't tell me you thought someone actually coupled yarn pile to a primary backing. Do you still believe in the Iranian tooth fairy too? That's just what Alan Thicke told children to hide the horrifying conditions at his carpet slaughterhouses in Boise, giants chained in place so robotic unicorn "caretakers" could harvest their skin layers with oversized cheese graters. Bit by bit, while the giants were still alive.

Like the Metropolitan Opera, the shrieks alone caused nightmares.

I suppose one could blame the carpet giants themselves… in a way. I knew for certain that Olivia de Havilland did. I mean, what did they think was going to happen when they grew such a thick, polymer skin sprouting a dense, plush weave of synthetic hairs? They probably should have counted themselves lucky that wall-to-wall carpeting didn't come out sooner. You wouldn't hear gratitude from them though, mostly you just heard screaming.

Still, the hardwood floor fad *was* less cruel.

Though, hardwood and stone tile could leave the old tootsies somewhat cold in the morning. People were moving to heated floors to take care of that, but it was still expensive, and by no means universal. Some people even objected to that technology.

Given the number of elves we had to kill in order to pump their naturally-heated blood throughout to accomplish it, I guess I could see why.

The Secret to Cessation of Desire Is to Use Real Butter in the Crust and Never Wear Wyatt Earp after Labor Day

I dreamed there was a green Buddha statue in my room when I was two. I don't remember where it came from, but I wasn't dreaming. Also, it wasn't really a Buddha statue. It was actually Jim Gaffigan.

He was green though.

For the longest time, he'd talk to me about Hot Pockets. I told him they wouldn't be invented until the eighties so he needed to cut that crap out. That's when he'd get violent. He said he didn't spend all those nights washing carburetors for electric cars to afford tuition to Cal Tech just to be lectured about time continuity by a two-year-old.

And he really didn't. M.I.T. was his alma mater, and they actually paid him to go. Had to, it was the only way to shore up their full-contact vinegar-and-oil style Croatian league dominoes team. They were slaughtered without him, and his test scores were going to do wonders for their *Auto Body Monthly* college ranking standings.

Schools do a lot for that sort of thing.

Except, it was really more of a seventeenth-century Trappist monastery than a school. The snare traps were a dead giveaway, particularly the ones labeled "property of a seventeenth-century Trappist monastery." That's pretty hard to argue against, though they were hoping Jim would try.

But he spent all his time arguing about Hot Pockets instead. They were even less relevant then than when I was two, being even further from being invented.

Truth be told, that's how Jim ended up in my bedroom. He went as the Buddha for a Guy Fawkes Day interpretive circumcision costume party and his get-up was a bit too good. On the lam from the resulting administrative hearings and the associated F.B.I. investigation, my bedroom was the natural hiding spot.

He certainly wasn't the first one.

Though, it was really more the Columbia Record and Tape Club than the F.B.I., and the Columbia Record and Tape Club was more accurately referenced as the editorial board for the irregular Sunday issue of *The New Yorker* special printed on the back of laminated Campbell's tomato soup labels.

Is it any wonder Jim got violent when pressed?

Hernández de Biedma Owes Me a Weekend

I wish I hadn't mixed up the assembly instructions for my IKEA BILLY bookshelf with the cooking steps on that box of Kraft Macaroni & Cheese. It blew my whole Sunday, and I had to start keeping my books buried in individual spots in the yard like the squirrels. Maybe I'd be more careful next time, or start getting my shelves at Walmart instead.

The boiling wasn't so bad. The shelves got soggy and smelled like old paste, but you have to expect that kind of thing. The trouble really started when I stirred the parts packet in with a quarter cup of milk and a pat of low-fat butter. Next thing I knew, I'd joined Hernando de Soto's 1539 expedition to North America.

What are the odds of that?

I was supposed to be finding him a land route to a package of Chinet salad plates, but he wasn't really buying: "It's over there. Just take a left." If it hadn't been for the as-of-yet unborn ghost of Ronald Reagan's midwife and a lucky misplacing of the expedition's crates of Manifest Destiny, I probably wouldn't have made it out alive.

Though…if I'd known I was going to end up working as a peanut wrangler for a marmot circus in Civil War-era Mexico City, maybe I would have told the Gipper's helper to hold off. Oh well, live and learn I suppose. At least De Soto never figured out who kept swiping his Zagnut bars whenever he was off pretending to be the sun god yet again.

Luckily, the circus decided to go on the road and, coincidentally enough, one of the planned stops was in modern-day Boulder. I simply hopped off at that point (unfortunately resulting in the deaths of seventeen deaf harpists) and took a bus, which worked out well since moments later Neil deGrasse Tyson flattened all the marmots with a meteor as part of an elaborate practical joke to impress Jody Foster. She laughed but didn't really go for it, and I already didn't end up getting home until seven.

An entire Sunday down the drain, and I had to be up early the next day to start my new job electroplating hobos for the Mattress King. Hopefully, everything goes okay with the mac and cheese when I give that a try.

It's the cheesiest.

Acknowledgments

It's likely that the acknowledgments section of this book would be one of the biggest pieces. It certainly would be if I could possibly remember to thank all the people who influenced this book. There's just no way, but I have to at least try to do my best…and I'd certainly have to start with Fred's wine.

You see, my friend Fred once tried to make strawberry wine at home. According to what he told me, he screwed it up pretty good. Instead of strawberry wine, it smelled and tasted like a high alcohol version of almond extract. It was foul. It burned. The stuff yielded terrible drunks and some of the worst hangovers I'd ever seen. He tried giving it out as gifts and people gave it back. A pair of my sneakers fell apart, something with the glue degrading after I'd spilled some on them. I, of course, told him I'd take all he'd give. I was one of only two people I knew who were enthused about drinking it, and I think I may be the only person who drank four bottles of the stuff in one evening. I don't drink anymore, but I certainly did then. And, one fair night while drinking Fred's wine, I started writing the oddest thing I'd ever written. It's now "There's a Rabbit Living Under My Kitchen Sink. . . .," but at the time it was just f*#<in' weird.

I sat on that piece for years, fiddling with it once in a while. Conversations with people like Natasha Kessler and Joseph Michael Owens at the University of Nebraska MFA in Writing led me to keep going with it, and with other similar pieces. I had no idea what I thought I was trying to do, but other pieces came and I started to do *something*.

And that's when I ran into Jon Konrath. I had this really strange idea for a piece that ended up as "Ideas: Where to Get Them and What to Do When They Won't Leave" (for which I should also thank my wife for handling the trick-or-treaters that Halloween evening as I was sitting writing the initial draft of the story on our coffee table instead), and a place called *Paragraph Line* actually ended up taking it, no one else even having the slightest idea what to do with these things (one fine journal remarked, upon me trying to submit "There's a Rabbit Living Under My Kitchen Sink. . . ." as a poem, "We love this. We couldn't possibly publish it."). My first reaction was shock. I wondered who the hell this Jon Konrath person was and why the hell he would accept something like that. That led to an interest in his work, as well as showing me all kinds of possibilities for what I was doing, as well entire segments of the writing world I was unaware of where other similarly interesting authors and writing were to be found. It was instrumental and foundational.

Then I attended a night of the Fbomb Flash Fiction reading series in Denver when I heard Robert Vaughan and Meg Tuite were going to be there. I was a regular attendee after what I heard. Nancy Stohlman curates the series and I was already familiar with her flash work through the incredible and innovative flash novel *The Monster Opera*, so I knew I needed to be there. Sure enough, the kind of space and encouragement I found there from Nancy and other amazing writers such as Steven Dunn, Hillary Leftwich, and many more really got me going, and took me to some astounding places…as you can hopefully see if you've already read this book.

This is even before FLASHNANO and all the prompts and encouragement Nancy put forth as part of that. The 2015 year of that is what really got me seriously thinking that this could really be a collection someday, and the 2016 year is what made it a real possibility. As vast bulk of the pieces of this book came from that, written on buses, in bed, in my office, in my living room, in Paris, on planes, in Vietnam, in London, and more. This book would be nowhere without all of that.

And, of course, there are the presses that were willing to publish some of these pieces over the years (in no particular order): *Paragraph Line; Rooster Republic Press; Cease, Cows; Used Gravitrons; Smashed Cat Magazine; Thumbnail; Apocrypha and Abstractions; Pure Slush; Truth Serum Press; Blue Five Notebook; Connotation Press; Five 2 One Magazine; Flash Frontier;* and *The Harpoon Review.* Immense thanks and gratitude from me to all of them, always.

But what about my parents who gave me both whatever (being generous) is slightly off-kilter in my brain and a psyche

jammed full of such disparate cultural elements as *Scooby-Doo,
Monty Python's Flying Circus*, Barbara Mandrell, Richard
Nixon, *Bloom County, Leonard Peltier, The Fabulous Furry
Freak Brothers, The Lord of the Rings, Groo the Wanderer,*
and so on? What about the freshman kids in my Latin class
when I was in eighth grade who were really weirded out but
still didn't kill me as I laughed hysterically while drawing
more oranges falling on Imelda Marcos sitting in a chair while
a cockroach version of Carmen Miranda danced around her on
my notebook? The debts are many, impossible to remember,
and connected to this book in strangely inexplicable ways. I'll
just have to say "thanks, everybody."

So, thanks, everybody.

Previous Publications

(some in earlier forms)

"90% of All Sourdough Turtles Break Apart in the Water on Their Very First Trip to the Sea" published February 15, 2017 in *True Truth Serum Vol. 1* from *Truth Serum Press*.

"Big Wheel Keeps on Turning, Little Wheel Abandoned Its Spouse and Children to Pursue Its Dreams of Becoming a Part-Time Mime in Spain" published January 22, 2017 in *Five 2 One Magazine*'s #thesideshow.

"Michael Rennie Was There the Day I Forgot my Bus Pass, But He Told Me Which Metro Line Went to the Ziegfeld Follies" published November 28, 2016 in issue #26 of *The Harpoon Review*.

"Ten-Gallon Hats Full of Cottage Cheese and the Grassroots Movement to Free K" published December 13, 2016 in *Freak Pure Slush Vol. 13*.

"Continental Breakfasts Sound Fancy so You Don't Realize It's a God Damned Muffin and You Should Have Just Gone to Tim Hortons" published September 25, 2016 in the September/Motel issue of *Flash Frontier*.

"Turns Out The Pizza Hut BOOK IT! Program Was Not for Fleeing Tax Evasion Charges" published September 22, 2016 as part of the cake theme at *Pure Slush*.

"In the Beginning, Good Always Overpowered Taxidermied Chipmunks and Free Frosting Wednesdays at Applebee's" published August 23, 2016 in *Summer Pure Slush Vol. 12*.

"Lord Rutherford's Gold Foil Disco Suits Were a Big Hit in Vegas But the Beryllium Earrings Were Simply Gaudy" published as part of the mirror theme June 15, 2016 at *Pure Slush*.

"Tony Robbins Told Fred to Follow Others' Dreams Instead of His Own Because They Thought Bigger" published June 10, 2016 in *tall…ish Pure Slush Vol. 11*.

"Polident Commercials for Indentured Servitude" published May 15, 2016 in Issue V, Volume VII of *Connotation Press*.

"Exxon Stole My Oatmeal" published May 15, 2016 in Issue V, Volume VII of *Connotation Press*.

"Deliberately Missing Henry Kissinger" published May 15, 2016 in Issue V, Volume VII of *Connotation Press*.

"Marc Summers Instigated the Bloods and Crips War so He Deserves Everything He Gets" published March 23, 2016 as part of the suit theme at *Pure Slush*.

"Hernández de Biedma Owes Me a Weekend" published May 4, 2016 in the Spring Quarterly (May 2016 / 16.4) issue of *Blue Five Notebook*.

"To Kill a Mokkingbird II — Kill Harder by Ahrrper Leeeeee" published February 5, 2015 in *Cease, Cows*.

"The Philosophical Problem of Original Jam" published July 16, 2015 in *Apocrypha and Abstractions*.

"Somebody Misplaced Montana" published in Issue 17 (September 2014) of *Used Gravitrons*.

"The Las Vegas Strip Disappeared This Morning" published September 9, 2014 *Smashed Cat Magazine*.

"I Contemplate the Humble Potato" published April 14, 2014 at *Cease, Cows*.

"Benjamin Franklin Was Pissing on My Apartment Building Door" published in *Thumbnail 5*.

"There's a Rabbit Living Under My Kitchen Sink..." published January 3, 2014 in *Paragraph Line*.

"Kidnapping with Margaret Thatcher" published in Rooster Republic Press's flagship bizarro anthology *Tall Tales with Short Cocks Vol. 4*.

"Ideas: Where to Get Them and What to Do When They Won't Leave" published July 9, 2012 in *Paragraph Line*.

Biography

David S. Atkinson is the author of *Apocalypse All the Time*, *Not Quite so Stories* (2016 Best Book Awards Finalist Fiction: Short Story & and 2017 Nebraska Book Awards Winner), *The Garden of Good and Evil Pancakes* (2015 National Indie Excellence Awards finalist in humor), and *Bones Buried in the Dirt* (2014 Next Generation Indie Book Awards finalist, First Novel <80K). He is a Staff Reader for *Digging Through The Fat* and his writing appears in *Literary Orphans, Flash Frontier, Atticus Review*, and others. His writing website is http://davidsatkinsonwriting.com/.

www.ingramcontent.com/pod-product-compliance
Lightning Source LLC
Chambersburg PA
CBHW050344190726
48284CB00007BB/2146